the séance

the séance

IAIN LAWRENCE

delacorte press

Published by Delacorte Press
an imprint of Random House Children's Books
a division of Random House, Inc.
New York

This is a work of fiction. All incidents and dialogue, and all characters with the exception of some well-known historical and public figures, are products of the author's imagination and are not to be construed as real. Where real-life historical or public figures appear, the situations, incidents, and dialogues concerning those persons are fictional and are not intended to depict actual events or to change the fictional nature of the work. In all other respects, any resemblance to persons living or dead is entirely coincidental.

Text copyright © 2008 by Iain Lawrence
Illustration pages 76 and 243 copyright © 2008 by Iain Lawrence
Illustrations pages 213 and 223 copyright © 2008 by Darlene Mace

Delacorte Press and colophon are registered trademarks of
Random House, Inc.

Visit us on the Web! www.randomhouse.com/kids

Educators and librarians, for a variety of teaching tools, visit us at
www.randomhouse.com/teachers

Library of Congress Cataloging-in-Publication Data
Lawrence, Iain.
   The seance / Iain Lawrence.—1st ed.
     p. cm.
   Summary: In 1926, magician Harry Houdini arrives in the city to perform magic and to expose fraudulent mediums but thirteen-year-old Scooter King, who works for his mother making her seances seem real, needs Houdini's help to solve a murder.
   ISBN 978-0-385-73375-5 (trade)—ISBN 978-0-385-90392-9 (glb)
   [1. Spiritualists—Fiction. 2. Magicians—Fiction. 3. Murder—Fiction.
   4. Houdini, Harry, 1874–1926—Fiction. 5. Mystery and detective stories.] I. Title.
PZ7.L43545Sea 2008
[Fic]—dc22   2007027994

The text of this book is set in 12-point Goudy.

Book design by Kenny Holcomb

Printed in the United States of America

10 9 8 7 6 5 4 3 2 1

First Edition

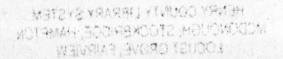

in memory of
Jane Jordan Browne

WEDNESDAY, JUNE 2, 1926

ADMIRAL BYRD CIRCLES NORTH POLE
FLAGPOLE SITTER TOPS FIFTEEN DAYS
SCIENTIFIC AMERICAN TESTS
 LOCAL MEDIUM

At five minutes to midnight, a stranger arrived for the séance. He came out of the hot summer darkness and tapped three times on the door.

The sitters were at their places, all four around the table. My mother was dressing in her bedroom. So I was the one who answered the knock. Scooter King, thirteen, I saw the Stranger in.

He was standing under the porch light, like a big moth in a rumpled overcoat, holding his hat and a bamboo cane. His hair was silver, his mustache gray, his spectacles thick and round. Behind the lenses of those cheaters, his eyes were almost yellow.

He spoke in a soft and mumbly voice. "I'm not too late, I hope. For the sitting, I mean." From the bowl of his hat he pulled out a scrap of newspaper. He showed me the advertisement that he'd circled in black.

1

"This *is* the proper place, isn't it?" asked the Stranger.

"Sure. Come in," I said.

The guy was a chump. He tried to take off his coat without putting down his cane, so he got himself in such a tangle that I had to unhook him from his own clothes. Then he gave me his things, and I led him into the tiny room that my mother called the vestibule but was really a closet with the shelves ripped out. Inside was a lamp, a wicker chair, and a spindly table that would shake if someone looked at it too hard. Piled on the tabletop were a stack of books, a candle and matches, and an ashtray shaped like a turtle. Under all that stuff, the table looked more crowded than Noah's ark, but the widgets were there for a reason.

"Madam King is waiting," I said. "If you could write out a question for the spirits, I—"

"That's not necessary," said the Stranger. He patted his mustache, smoothing its ends. "I have only one wish, and that's to hear from my poor Annie."

"Of course." I turned away and dumped the Stranger's stuff on the chair. His eyes had changed color in the lamplight, reflecting the red from the roses that sprawled on the wallpaper. It gave me the heebie-jeebies to look at them. "Please follow me," I said.

We went down the hall and into the séance room. Mr. Stevenson twisted round in his chair to squint at us over his narrow bifocals. That week he'd turned seventy-one. He had been a drummer boy in the Civil War; he had met President Lincoln. But he was still the youngest at the table. If their ages had been added together, it would have been more than three hundred years. After every séance, I had to open the windows to blow out the old-people smell.

I got a chair for the Stranger and sat him at the end of the table. Of course I made sure that his back was toward the huge wardrobe that stood against the wall. Mr. Stevenson leaned forward and shouted at him, "Are you a believer, sir?"

"I believe what I see," said the Stranger.

"Well, see *this*," said Mr. Stevenson, bristling like a porcupine. But his wife calmed him down. She patted his hand and told the Stranger, "Henry's hoping to contact Paul Revere tonight. You see, Henry's a bug about Paul Revere, and—"

"I'm not a *bug*," said Mr. Stevenson. "I'm *interested*."

"Oh, he only knows more about Paul Revere than anyone alive." Mrs. Stevenson smiled at her husband. "He's frightened that a nonbeliever might block the spirits. They do that, you know."

"I assure you, I will block no spirits," said the Stranger.

I left them at the table, went out, and shut the door. Then I sprinted down the hall to the vestibule and snatched the Stranger's hat from the chair.

The sweatband was still warm. I peeled it away with my thumb, bending it back to look for a name underneath. When I found it, I smiled. The first initial was blurry from sweat, but the rest was easy to read.

J. Brown

I turned to the overcoat next. I rifled every pocket, but all I got was a hatcheck stub from the Limelight Club and a Chuckles candy wrapped in lint. But there was a hole in the right-hand pocket, so I groped through the lining and found two curious things. The first was a small metal ring, the second a sticky ball of lint and mold.

Now, this was the sort of puzzle that I liked to solve. By itself, the ring didn't seem important. But I figured if the green stuff was an old biscuit, then maybe the ring came from a dog tag. I imagined Mr. Brown stuffing his pockets with Chuckles and biscuits, picking up a leash, whistling for Annie. He wouldn't have been the first person to come to Madam King about a dead dog. It happened nearly every month, someone showing up to speak to a dog or cat—or even a budgie—that had gone along to Summerland.

But once I had made a mistake. An old lady had sat in that same chair in the vestibule, sobbing so loudly that I could hardly understand her. I figured she was talking about a dog called Rover, so my mother had held her hands and said that Rover was happy in the world beyond. "He chases rabbits all day long," she'd said. "I can see him right now, lying in long grass; yes, lying there licking himself." The old lady had let out a horrible shriek. She'd left in a huff, and I'd found Mother laughing in her chair, just sitting there crying with laughter. "It wasn't Rover," she'd said. "It was *Grover*, her husband."

Now I was as careful as I could be. I replaced the Stranger's things just where I'd found them—even the linted Chuckles—because there really were people so dishonest that they'd try to fool a medium. I hung the coat on a peg and went quickly through Mrs. Figg's handbag, looking for theater stubs and photographs. I was just starting on Mrs. Hardy's black purse when my mother came to the vestibule door.

I showed her the metal ring and the name inside the hat. "Are you sure that's a *J*? It looks like an *I*," she said. "Oh, darn you, Mr. Brown. Why can't you write your whole name, you bonehead?"

"Just call him Mr. Brown," I said. "Tell him Annie is happy. Annie doesn't want him to worry."

"Yes. That's good," said Mother.

She put on her shawl, sweeping it over her head. The cloth fluttered down on top of her red curls, and she tied the ends loosely below her chin. Then she smiled and touched my arm. "I don't know what I'd do without you, Scooty," she said.

I followed her to the door of the séance room. The gas lamps flared and fluttered as she went sweeping past them. She took her place at the head of the table. "Join hands, please," she said.

I could see that the Stranger had done it a hundred times. His hands slid into place, his fingers overlapping Mrs. Figg's.

"Never break the circle," said my mother. "No matter what you see or hear, don't ever let go. The circle contains the energy of the spirits. If it's broken, the shock can be fatal."

Well, it was all baloney. Just a lot of applesauce. But the old folks lapped it up. Mrs. Figg nodded gravely. Eighty years old—maybe more—she had a face like a weasel's. Her fingers were stiff and yellow, dotted with creepy liver spots. I always wanted to snap them off and play a game of dominos.

"The lights, please," said my mother.

I turned the valve slowly, so that the hiss of gas would fade like a ghostly whisper. It was Mother's idea to have gas in the séance room, and I thought it was the bee's knees. As the flames shrank away, shadows jumped and stretched. When I stepped out and closed the door, the room was blacker than a grave.

I could hear my mother starting the Lord's Prayer, the sitters mumbling along. She would follow it with her own prayer: "Protect us from the spirits," and all that jazz.

Altogether, she had to talk for about three minutes. It took me that long to reach the kitchen and get myself ready.

I put on my black smock, the hood and gloves. I got my reaching rods and balloons, turned off the lights, and opened the secret panel in the back of the wardrobe.

That thing was big enough to hide the real doorway. As I stepped inside it, I passed from the kitchen to the séance room. I could hear Mother humming herself into her trance, so I parked my stuff in a corner of the wardrobe and cracked open the doors at the front. I squinted into the dark until I saw the blobs of green paint on the tambourine and the speaking trumpet. It was Cheever's Luminous Paint, so bright that I could see the heads and shoulders of the sitters silhouetted in its green glow. They looked like campers sitting round a crazy witches' fire.

My mother was running on all six now, warbling away at the top of her voice. There was a soft jingle from the tambourine, so I figured she had nudged the table with her knee. A moment later, there was a squeal of wood, and someone shouted, "The table's tilting!" It fell back with a bang, the tambourine jangling.

Suddenly, there was silence.

A cave at the middle of the earth couldn't have been more quiet. I heard a fly buzzing round the room. I even heard it tick up against the ceiling.

Mother kept it that way for a good minute. She kept it so long that I could almost *feel* the silence, like a thing that was in the room. Then, from the dark, came three sharp knocks that brought a cry from Mrs. Hardy. Every séance began with those three strikes of the rapper, a signal from Mother that her left hand was free from the circle. Already, she had managed to draw the hands of her neighbors so close together that she could touch them both with the fingers of her right hand.

Now she rang her little hand bell. It was the sort of bell that rich people used to call for their butlers. Tonight it summoned spirits.

"We have opened a portal to the other world," said Mother. "The spirits are among us."

"The tambourine!" shouted Mrs. Hardy. "Oh, mercy, it's moving!"

I could see its band of green paint slide away from the Stranger. It shot up in the air like a little comet, flying nearly to the ceiling before it crashed onto the floor in front of me. I picked it up as I walked out of the wardrobe, swinging it in huge circles so that the green paint seemed to wheel through the darkness. I dropped it back on the table with a jarring rattle. Mrs. Figg gasped.

My mother's voice was now deep and unearthly. "I have a message," she said. "It's for a Mr. Brown. Does that make sense to anyone?"

"That's for me," said the Stranger, in the dark.

"I'm getting the sense of an Anne, or an Annie," said Mother. "I'm getting a sense of contentment. Of happiness." She fell silent for a moment, then began again. "There's a feeling of love for this Mr. Brown."

I kept walking round the table. With a wave of my hand I sent a draft of air against Mrs. Figg's long neck. She twitched in her chair. I used my reaching rod to hook on to the eyelet in the middle of the speaking trumpet.

"This feeling of love is strong," said Mother. "Annie doesn't wish to see Mr. Brown unhappy. She is with him at this moment, hovering just above him."

I touched the Stranger, very lightly, on the top of his head. Then I lifted the trumpet, and the long cone of metal seemed to float in the air, light as a bubble. Dangling above the heads of the sitters, it turned a full circle as I brought the thin end to my lips. I whispered through it, "We still live."

I aimed that trumpet toward the Stranger, then high above the table, so that the words would seem to come from the very air. "Death is a door, not a wall," I whispered.

For each of the sitters, my mother brought a message. There was one from Mrs. Figg's great-grandfather, another from Mrs. Hardy's baby girl, who'd died before she'd even learned to talk. While Mother trotted them out, I kept swooping in to the table, brushing faces and necks and arms. I made the ladies shriek.

When everyone had received a message or two and poor Mrs. Hardy was sobbing away, Mother called for her spirit guide. "We ask you to lead us through the world of shadows," she said. "Please come."

She gave the little bell two rings. Her voice changed to a child's—a very young girl's. "It's dark in here," she said.

I always shivered when that voice came floating from the blackness. My mother made it so clear and perfect that I could picture the girl standing in the room. She would be small and blond and pretty. But her skin would be sickly white and cold as ice. I grabbed my flask from the wardrobe and began splashing drops of water round the table. I made sure to sprinkle the Stranger.

"It's lovely and dark in here," said the girlish voice. "I'm afraid of light, you know."

Mrs. Figg whispered to the Stranger. "That's Dorothy. She drowned on the *Titanic*."

"I'm lonely," said Dorothy. "Is there anyone on this side you'd like to talk to?"

"Yes!" cried Mr. Stevenson. "Paul Revere! Please, can we speak with the spirit of Paul Revere?"

"Let me see," said Dorothy. "I thought he was— Oh, yes, I think I see him now. He's very distant now, no brighter than a star. But I believe he's coming this way."

I was ready, waiting at the wardrobe. I made the sound of hoofbeats with my hands, drumming on the wooden panel. I made it so faint at first that it was hardly there. Then I let the sound grow louder and faster.

"Yes, he's coming!" said Mr. Stevenson. "That must be old Hooker he's riding!"

I hunched beside the wardrobe, pounding out the hoof-beats. The trumpet was wedged in place, its end at my lips. I breathed the snorting breaths of the galloping horse.

"Stop!" shouted my mother, in Dorothy's voice. It was as though the little girl was frightened of being trampled. "I don't like this!" she shrieked. "I want him to go back right now!"

But I kept thumping and pounding.

This wasn't how we'd planned it. I was supposed to walk slowly round the room with a bit of painted cheesecloth on my head. I was supposed to whisper about old Boston and the tea party and any blah-blah that came to my mind. But this was better. This was all to the mustard!

The phantom hooves made a furious sound. When old Hooker seemed to thunder right through the wall and into the room, I wailed through the trumpet: "The British are coming! The British are coming!"

The wardrobe shook; the table shook. Mrs. Figg drew down her head, as though Paul Revere was leaping his horse right above her. Then the hoofbeats and the ghostly cries faded away, and the rider vanished again into his world of shadows.

"That is all!" shouted my mother in her own voice. Dorothy was gone, her spirit forgotten. "The portal has closed. I see no more!"

I had to hurry then. I slipped back through the wardrobe, dumped my things on the counter, pulled off my smock and gloves. When I reached the doors to the séance room, Mother was hollering for the lights to be lit. I threw the doors open and saw her glaring at me.

I had never seen her so angry, not even on the night when I'd dropped Cleopatra's face. Mrs. Stevenson had found the painted handkerchief on the floor and had nearly become a nonbeliever. Mother had managed to laugh about *that*. But now she rose from her chair and swished right past me. "You'll be sorry," she whispered. "This time you've gone too far."

Mr. Stevenson stood up slowly. He pushed his chair to the table. "Well, that was interesting," he said.

I knew the old socks was hard to please, but I was disappointed that he wasn't a bit more excited than that. Everyone else was over the moon. "Can you believe it, Henry?" said his wife. "Paul Revere rode right through this very room." She felt the air with her hands. "I could smell his horse, you know. I saw its eyes. They were burning!"

"He touched me," said Mrs. Figg, with a little shiver. "I felt his ghostly hand."

They left the house bubbling with excitement. The Stranger put both his hands round one of my mother's and crushed a five-dollar bill in her palm. Then he went out swinging his cane like a dancer, as though he'd grown younger by twenty years.

Mother watched him go down the steps and across the lawn. "He seems a nice man," she said. "That wig makes him look older, though."

"He was wearing a *wig*?" I said.

"Why, sure. No one has hair as silver as that." She closed the door, then smiled at me. "Look, I'm sorry I got angry. Come give me a hug, Scooty."

She pulled me off balance. I toppled forward, stiff as a stick. Even with nobody there to see us, I was embarrassed. I thought I was too old to be hugging my mother. But, in a way, I didn't mind.

"You're so cold!" she said. "You're not getting sick, are you?"

"No, Mom," I said.

It was strange. She was the medium. So why was I the one who felt chilled and uneasy, as though something terrible had come into our lives?

2

THURSDAY, JUNE 3, 1926

WORLD'S FAIR DRAWS CROWDS IN PHILLY
WOMAN DIES IN DANCE MARATHON
SHOCKING DISPLAY AT THE ORPHEUM

Every morning I had Pep for breakfast. I ate it from the same black bowl, using the same red-handled spoon, as I watched Mother snip away at the morning paper.

She went at it with a pair of scissors, starting at the back. She read the obituaries first, cutting out anything with a prospect. Then she moved forward to "The Man in the Moon," the gossip column that sounded like a whole lot of sappy telegrams strung together: *Has Pamela Dukes gone Cupid for Carleton Twigg? Couple seen arm-in-arming through the lobby of the Grande.*

This morning, she was more happy than usual. There had been good pickings in the death notices. "Two widows this morning," she said as I poured out the Pep. "And one old bird left childless."

When I finished eating, she gave me the clippings. I went to the desk in the corner and rolled back the top.

I pulled out the city directory, flipped it open, and started looking for addresses. To each of the widows, and to the poor man who'd lost his son, I sent the same yellow card.

MADAM KING

IN TOUCH WITH THE SPIRIT WORLD

I have received a message from a dearly departed who wishes to contact you. This may be an urgent matter. Come as soon as possible.

"Planting beans," said Mother, at the table. "That's what we're doing, Scooty, isn't it? Maybe one of those cards will be the magic bean that grows into a money tree."

"Sure," I said. She never gave up hope. We had planted a heap of beans but had never grown a money tree.

I put a code number on each card, matching it to the obituary. I filed the death notices and the cuttings from "The Man in the Moon." They would give Mother plenty of things to "see" at her séances.

"Oh, Scooter!" she cried suddenly. "Come and look at this. Quick!"

I went back to the table and leaned over her shoulder. There was a huge headline at the top of the page: "Houdini Arrives in the City." There was a picture of him stepping off the train, glaring down from the door of his Pullman car. He looked mean, like a gunfighter on his way to a shootout.

"I hope he's not coming for *me*," said Mother. "That

man . . . he's a *disease*. There won't be a medium left in the country when he's done."

Harry Houdini hunted mediums. He made a business—and a sport as well—of exposing the fakes.

"Do you think he's heard of me?" said Mother. "Oh, I couldn't live with it if he came after me."

She covered her face with her hands, and I kept reading the paper. I saw that Houdini would be playing at the Orpheum for two weeks. His famous Burmese Torture Tank was being put on display. Before his first show on Friday, he would escape from a straitjacket while hanging from a beam high above the street. I didn't tell Mother, but I wanted to see it all. No one in the world was more famous than Harry Houdini.

Mother used her scissors to hack at the picture. She stabbed it seven times. "Take that, you horrible man," she said. Then she ripped the page in half, exposing the one underneath. "Oh, look. *That's* why he's here," she said. "See, Scooter?"

There was a longer headline on that new page: "Russian Spook Will Claim Prize, Says Dr. Wiseman."

It sounded mysterious, but I knew what it meant. The "Russian spook" was Viktor Valerian, the most renowned medium in the city. The prize was twenty-five hundred dollars, and Dr. Wiseman was one of the men who could give it away. Both he and Houdini were members of the *Scientific American* committee that was traveling all over the country, searching for a medium with genuine powers. Three times in the last year, Dr. Wiseman had announced that he'd found one, and the committee had started trials. But all three times, Houdini had swooped in to show up the medium as a fraud.

"Well, this is the end for Viktor. No one tricks Houdini," said Mother. "Not no one, no how. Houdini will shake out that Bolshevik like an old carpet."

"Maybe Viktor's on the level," I said. "Maybe he'll be the first one with real powers."

"What about me?" said Mother sharply. "Don't I see things before they happen? Don't I sense disaster when it's coming?"

"Well, sometimes," I said, "but—"

"Of course it's only *sometimes*," she said. "You can't turn miracles on and off like a lightbulb, you know. People are so busy these days—oh, so busy with their mah-jongg and their crossword puzzles and their dancing marathons and all—that they don't have time to sit around and wait for a miracle. So I give them what they want; it makes them happy. Dollars to donuts Viktor Valerian does the same thing."

I took my bowl to the sink, smiling to myself. Through every séance for nearly two years, I had worked the reaching rods and spirit lights, the painted faces and shimmering gauze. But Mother could somehow ignore all of that. She really believed that she talked with the dead.

"The world's not the same anymore. That's the trouble,"

she said. "Everything changed fourteen years ago, when the big ship went down."

The *Titanic*, she meant. Mother couldn't talk about the *Titanic* without getting all sappy.

"I'll tell you, Scooter. That April night when the cold water closed over the big ship—that was the end of old money," she said. "After that, you didn't have to be born rich. You could *make* yourself rich; even a Bolshevik could. All you have to do now is sit long enough on a flagpole, or dance the Charleston till you nearly drop dead. Do anything crazy, and people start throwing money your way."

It was Mother's dream to be rich. She wanted to sail to England and tour haunted castles, to hold séances for Sir Arthur Conan Doyle.

"Twenty-five hundred bucks," she said, staring at the paper. "Do you know what we could do with that kind of money?"

"Buy a new auto," I said.

"Small potatoes!" she cried. "We could buy two or three autos. And a fancy house. And a cottage, and a gardener. We could even buy a yacht."

"You don't want a yacht," I said.

"No, but I want to buy one." She made a pouty face, then reached out and flicked the paper. "Gee, it isn't fair." Her red curls were shaking. "I thought *I* was the one who would get that prize. You know, I had a little dream?"

I didn't answer. This was the first time that Mother had

talked of winning the *Scientific American* prize, and she was giving me the whoops and jiggles.

"Viktor's only been a medium for four years," she said. "Not even that, 'cause he only bought his crummy old castle in twenty-one, and he wasn't a medium then. Do you know how long I've been at it?"

"Yes, Mom. Eleven years."

"And then some!"

Well, it was eleven years and two months. Her "Certificate of Ordination" hung in the vestibule, and the date at the bottom was April 3, 1915. It was a gaudy thing with ribbons and cherubs, naming her an official reverend in the Church of Spirituality. She had paid five dollars to get it.

"I know I've told you a thousand times, but I started with nothing but a Ouija board," she said. "Your father and I, we made a killing. But I never cheated people. I never suckered them into spirit banks or magnetism, and I sure didn't steal their life savings. Not like that Bolshevik. The big phony baloney."

"What do you mean?"

"Oh, Russian, smushin'," said Mother. "To him, the Far East is New Jersey. He's a bootlegger from the Bronx; that's what they say. I think I read it in 'The Man in the Moon.' It was gin money that fixed up that old castle; Viktor's just moved into a different kind of spirit business now. He's as fake as they come. I should unmask him myself!"

She turned suddenly in her chair. She looked at me with the particular smile that made men blush. "Say, Scooty, he has a séance every Thursday, doesn't he? Don't you think it's time we took it in?"

I thought that was a swell idea. Viktor's house had been abandoned for years when he bought it. On account of its turrets and things, people called it "the castle." All my life, I'd seen it looming above the downtown streets, its windows black and empty. But I had never been inside.

"When you've finished with the dishes, go start old Stanley," said Mother.

She meant our auto, the old Stanley Steamer that looked more like a carriage than a motorcar. I hated it worse than I hated broccoli. I had to spend half an hour getting the boiler filled, the burner lit, the steam pressure up. Then we had to sit on top like hillbillies on a wagon. When we finally puttered away in a whirl of steam, the time was well after noon.

Mother thought she looked flashy in her goggles and hat, with a yellow scarf fluttering behind her. But I felt embarrassed as we motored through the downtown streets. All around us were the fancy Packards and the black Fords, their gasoline engines purring like big cats. I watched for horse-drawn carts, gloating each time I saw one, because it meant that we weren't—after all—the most pitiful thing on the road.

We passed right under Viktor's house. It stood on the steepest part of the bluff, overhanging the rock like Dracula's castle. On either side, spidery staircases crept to the top of the bluff, zigzagging back and forth. I kept turning in my seat, looking back at that house until it was hidden behind the buildings. Then we made the sharp curve at Three Corners and started up the long hill to the Uplands, doubling back along the top of the cliff. Soon swanky houses blocked the view, and huge trees made tunnels with their branches. At Viktor's castle, a pair of stone lions guarded the entrance. They weren't much bigger than alley cats, but each stood on a stone pillar, holding a paw in the air.

We drove up a long driveway, past a pond and a fountain, into a covered entrance. There were seven autos parked under the roof. We had to climb twenty steps to get to the front door.

"Doesn't it make you just turn green?" said Mother, reaching for the bell. "I bet a butler shows us in."

She rang three times before the door opened. Then I looked into a dark hall that was full of shadows, at a man who might have been a shadow himself. If he was the butler, he must have been buttling since the Civil War.

He sat in a tall tricycle chair, all covered with blankets that were marked with checks and tartans. I could see the toes of his shoes, one of his hands, and the tip of his nose, and that was all. He had a stocking cap pulled down on his head and a pair of dark glasses on his eyes. He seemed shriveled, hunched, and bent, and I figured he was older than King Tut.

"Name?" he said. He sounded like a frog.

"Madam King. And Scooter," said my mother.

He twitched a finger below the blankets, pointing to a box on a little table. "The master works by donation."

Mother put in some money. The man said, "Come this way."

He didn't move a muscle that I could see. But the chair spun round and carried him off, past a tiny elevator with its cage drawn shut, down a black passage into the house. Rubber tires rumbling, the chair moved with the hum of an electric motor. We started after it.

The house was a labyrinth. I looked north through one window, across wide gardens to the neighboring house, and east from the next, over the roof of the Orpheum to Victory Square. I could see the flagpole sitter, then in his seventeenth day, on his platform at the top of the pole.

We followed the shriveled man to a big, black room. The floor, the ceiling, and every wall were painted black. But there were dozens and dozens of lights—hanging from the ceiling, fixed to the walls, standing on the floor and the tables. The room was blazing bright.

There were curiosities on every shelf and table: a toy piano; a child's top; seashells and dried starfish; a telephone with a candlestick holder. In the middle of the room was Viktor's cabinet. It was made of wood and cloth—eight feet square and eight feet high—and it stood on a platform that itself stood on eight short legs, so the cabinet was raised six inches above the floor, and reached nearly to the ceiling. Its narrow door was open, and I could see a wooden chair inside, fixed in place by chains and locks.

My mother had never used a materializing cabinet. She made out that they were nonsense, that only a fraud ever needed one. But that was a lot of applesauce. She never used a cabinet for the same reason that she never went into our vestibule. Closed-in spaces scared her half to death.

I had studied the cabinets in the catalog from Bishop's Supply, where Mother bought her luminous paint and ecto-plasm. I knew where to look for secret pockets and hidden doorways sewn into the walls. But I found nothing, though I searched everywhere. I even pretended to drop a coin so that I could get down on my knees and look under the cabi-net. Between the short legs, I could see the wall on the other side of the room.

I stood up again. I brushed my knees and my elbows. I turned around and looked up, and there was the Stranger.

He was standing just a few feet away, staring right at me with his weird eyes. In the black room, they now seemed darker. I pretended to wave to my mother and hurried toward the door.

Mother was sitting there, on a short sofa, beside an eld-erly man in a trench coat. I thought I had seen the guy be-fore but couldn't remember where. He was touching her sleeve, and she was laughing. She was shaking her hair, so the light sparkled on her curls.

"Oh, Scooter!" she said as I came up beside her. "This is Dr. Wiseman. He's a member of the *Scientific American* committee."

I remembered him then. I had never met the man, but I had seen his picture on the jackets of books. He had traveled all over the world, from séance to séance, writing about spiritualism. Now he had a mash on my mother; I could see that. It had taken him less than five minutes to fall head over heels for Madam King—not quite a record, but close. Mother didn't look like a vamp, but—wowzers!—she could vamp like nobody's business.

Dr. Wiseman stood up and shook my hand. He wasn't more than an inch or two taller than me. He was very fair and covered with freckles, with no beard or mustache at all. He looked like the stuffy sort of man who spent all his time at dull parties indoors. He was more polite than Emily Post. "A pleasure to meet you," he said.

"Is this where the committee holds its trials, sir?" I asked. "In this room?"

"Why, your mother asked me the very same thing," said Dr. Wiseman. He tipped his head a bit, as though he was hard of hearing. "Yes, this is the place. As I told your mother, our sessions must be conducted in private, or I would gladly invite you."

He gave me a friendly smile, then leaned over and whispered in Mother's ear. When she tipped back her head and laughed, I saw the flash of her teeth—made pink by smeared lipstick. "Oh, Dr. Wiseman!" she said, tossing up her hand.

Dr. Wiseman bowed and backed away. But there seemed to be magnets in the tips of his fingers, because they stuck on to Mother's wrist until the very last moment.

Just as they parted, I saw Viktor Valerian come into the room.

The Russian was a tall man with black hair, with a

pointed beard like the ace of spades. The room grew quiet the moment he appeared, with everyone staring at him like a roomful of statues. He glanced slowly round, then fixed his eyes on Mother. When he smiled, she blushed and turned away.

"Please take your places," he said. His voice was deep, his accent strange. He made a sharp clap with his hands. "Now. We must begin."

The chairs were arranged in rows at one end of the room, all facing the cabinet. Mother and I sat in the second row. I felt a prickling in my neck, looked back, and saw the Stranger nearly behind me. It made me so uneasy to have him there that I nudged my mother, then nodded for her to look.

"*I know*," she mouthed back. "*Ignore him.*"

Viktor didn't waste any time. He went straight to the cabinet, stooped through the entrance, and settled onto the chair. The chains that held it jingled and clanked. Without another look toward us, he closed the cabinet door and sealed himself inside.

It was strange that there was no one there to dim the lights, no one to see that the spectators stayed in their places. We all watched the cabinet as though it might lift up and float through the air.

For a long time, nothing happened. Then a table lamp went out, and another across the room. A chandelier darkened, then a floor lamp, and in a flickering rush all the others followed. In the darkness, a blue glow began to pulse faintly in the cabinet. It shone through the tiny gap around the door and out through the open top, casting a watery glow on the ceiling. Slowly, it grew brighter. Then it leapt up from the cabinet and hung shimmering in the air, like the flames of a campfire, but with no wood to fuel it.

In the light of that ghostly blue fire, things began to happen. The toy piano on its shelf played out a little song. We could see its keys depressing, but the music seemed to come from everywhere. We heard a guitar join in for a moment, until its strings made a sudden, sour note. Then it hurled up from the cabinet, spinning over the wall, and crashed onto the floor. Other things followed: a bunch of flowers; a lady's hat; a shower of confetti. Out came a red balloon that floated softly to the floor, only to rise again and return the same way.

My mother's eyes looked huge. She sat holding herself, as though the air was freezing. I took a glance back and saw an empty chair. The Stranger was gone.

Until then, I was nearly ready to believe that Viktor Valerian was on the level. But that empty chair spoiled it all. The Stranger, I thought, was Viktor's assistant. He had collected the gossip, then snuck away to work the blue light and the toy piano. I didn't understand how the stuff worked, but I meant to find out.

No one looked as I got out of my chair; nobody stopped me from leaving the room. The fossilized butler wasn't guarding the hall. I made my way toward the front door, but I wasn't halfway there when I heard it open. The hinges creaked, and someone went running out. I hurried round the twists and bends of the corridor but got lost along the way. When I reached the door, it was open. I ran out, across the porch, down the steps to the garden. I got a glimpse of a figure in a long coat vanishing round the corner of the mansion.

I went after him. I turned the same corner a moment later, only to find nothing but empty lawn, as perfect as a golfing green. The man might have gone in any direction: down the side of the house to the cliff, over the neighbor's hedge to the right, off to the orchards and a white gazebo at the edge of the swanky gardens. I gazed all around, at every place, before I thought of looking down.

There were shadows of footprints on the grass. The lawn was so perfectly cut, so short and tidy, that the marks of shoes were like puddles of darker green. But even as I looked, those puddles were evaporating. Bent blades of grass were straightening, the shadows disappearing.

I wished I was a tracker. I couldn't even tell for sure if I was looking at the toe or the heel of a shoe print. But a row of round holes drilled into the grass looked like the marks of a walking stick. It seemed to me that the long-coated man had crossed to a gate at the corner of the property. I ran after him, through the gate to a walking path, to the rickety stairs on the bluff.

From there I stared out at the city. I could see hundreds of autos, thousands of people, all milling around in the streets. It seemed hopeless to go down there and look for the

Stranger. I didn't even know for sure that he had taken the stairs; he might have gone in the other direction. I almost turned around and went back to the house. But something was going on.

The Orpheum was nearly right below me, and on the other side of the street was the Herald building, home of the morning paper. Between the buildings, a crowd was breaking apart. The big clump in the middle was dissolving, all the little pieces—the men in hats and coats—slowly trickling away in every direction. Whatever had happened down there, I guessed it had something to do with Houdini. I figured the famous Torture Tank had arrived.

I told myself that I had to follow the Stranger. But the real reason that I started down the steps was to see that thing, that Burmese Torture Tank. I made myself dizzy, turning all the corners in those stairs. At the bottom, I bent over with my hands on my knees, thinking I would pull a Daniel Boone right then and vomit on the sidewalk. But the feeling went away, and I hurried on. Not five minutes after I'd left the castle, I was pushing through the revolving door at the Orpheum.

The lobby was like a church—huge and quiet. The red carpet on the floor was thicker than seven regular carpets. There was a gurgling fountain, and huge chandeliers of glittering glass. High on a ladder, a man was hanging posters on the walls. And even the posters were enormous.

They were pictures of Harry Houdini, each one the size of a giant. There were Houdinis in handcuffs and leg irons, shirtless Houdinis with great muscles bulging. They all glowered right at me as I walked through the lobby.

Six high doors led into the auditorium. But a seventh door—just regular size—opened into an anteroom off the end of the lobby, and I could see in there the gleam and flash from Houdini's wonderful Burmese Torture Tank. That light drew me in like a moth.

I'd thought there would be crowds of people around it, but the room seemed deserted. I walked slowly up to the Torture Tank.

It was made of steel and glass. Around the top were bolts as thick as my arm, and chains and locks and catches. They all hung loose, because the lid had been taken off and was now leaning against the side of the tank. Spotlights shone up from the floor and down from the ceiling, making mirrors of the glass walls. I could see myself creeping forward, looking tiny and frightened in all that hugeness.

I wanted to look inside, to see where Houdini would hang upside down in the water-filled tank. I had seen pictures of him trapped between the iron spikes, bound with chains and locks. So I went right to the tank, cupped my hands on the glass, and peered between them.

What I saw made me scream.

Inside the tank was a dead man.

3

EXTRA!

ACTRESS GETS A BREAK

The dead man was upside down. I stared right into his face, and he stared back with white and bulging eyes.

I fell away in fright. I screamed again as another person appeared in front of me. I'd thought the room was empty, but suddenly a man was there, springing out from behind the tank. He swung at me with a stick, then bowled me over as he bolted for the door. I got only a glimpse of an old man in a long coat, with a white beard that streamed behind him like smoke.

I didn't know if he was the same man I had followed down the stairs. In a flash, he was gone, before I could get a second look. I heard the revolving doors hum and shudder. A motorcar blasted its horn. I was just starting to get up from the floor when someone else came into the room.

It was a girl in a flapper's dress, with fringes that slapped at her knees. She was chewing bubble gum. "Hey, what's going on?" she said. "What are you doing lying on the floor?"

I pointed at the Torture Tank. "There's a man in there," I said. "A dead man."

"Ah, baloney!" she said. But she went to the wall and flicked a switch that turned off the spotlights all at once.

Without the glare on the glass, I saw the dead man clearly. The Torture Tank was studded with iron spikes, like a cactus turned inside out. The man was snared among the metal points, and the way his arms and legs were twisted made me think of spaghetti twirled on a fork. He was a small man, middle-aged, with a toupee that had fallen away at the front and now dangled from his head by a bit of tape.

There was blood on the floor of the tank. It was dripping from the bowl of his toupee and from the tips of his hanging fingers.

"Jeepers creepers!" said the girl. "You know who that is? That's Herman Day."

"Who's Herman Day?" I asked.

"You're kidding me, right?" She chewed loudly, her gum smacking. "You never heard of Knight and Day?"

"Oh, Knight and *Day*! Yeah, sure I have." I could see she didn't believe me, but I wasn't lying. Knight and Day were comedians, so famous in vaudeville that even my mother had heard of them.

"I'm going to call Mr. Topper," said the girl. "So you better tell me what you're doing here."

"What are *you* doing here?" I countered.

"None of your beeswax," she said. "But if you must know, I work here. I'm an actress, who happens to be engaged temporarily as a hatcheck girl."

She went flouncing to the door and leaned out into the lobby. "Mr. Topper!" she shouted as loudly as she could. "Mr. Topper! You better come in here."

"Who's Mr. Topper?" I asked.

"The manager. He runs the joint." She came walking back across the room. Through the fringes on her dress, I saw the tops of her rolled-up stockings and flashes of her kneecaps. She went right to the Torture Tank and stood staring at Herman Day.

She didn't seem frightened or queasy. She looked through the glass with a curious expression, as though the dead man was a big pickle in a giant jar. The gum popped and snapped in her mouth.

"Wait till Mr. Topper sees this," she said. "He'll try to sound sorry, but inside he'll be tickled pink. Someone just saved old Tops a ton of trouble."

"What do you mean?" I asked.

"He was saying this morning that it was the end of the road for Herman. He was tired of fighting with the guy, and he was going to give him his pictures back."

"What pictures?"

"Use your bean; it's just an expression," she said. "Tops was going to give Herman the boot; that's what I meant. He

33

had to get rid of him fast, 'cause Houdini said he would never share a stage with a fink like Herman Day. Especially not on opening night."

"Really?"

"Yes. Really." She blew a pink bubble from her mouth, then sucked it back between her teeth. "Everyone hated Hermie."

"Like who?" I asked.

She laughed. "Like who didn't? Even Melvin Knight couldn't stand the guy. Herman was a pill."

It seemed awful to me that she was talking about a dead man that way, especially while his body hung upside down beside her, still dribbling blood. I didn't know Herman Day, but I sure felt sorry for him, if only because nobody else was going to. It made me sad that his white socks weren't the same height, that his bright little bow tie was a bit crooked on his collar. He sported gold cufflinks set with red jewels, but I could tell right away they had come from a dime store. I thought of him getting dressed that morning—polishing those crummy cufflinks, putting on that tie—as though he thought it would be any regular day.

I walked around the Torture Tank. I climbed up on the lid and looked down from above.

"What do you think you're doing now?" asked the hat-check girl.

"Just looking," I said. I could see the soles of Herman Day's shoes. They were scuffed and dusty. "I'm trying to figure out what happened."

"Ya don't say." She put her hands on her hips and blew another bubble. "So, you in the Riddle Club or something?"

"No!" I said. The Riddle Club was a bunch of girls. It was just stories for girls.

Into the room came a man in a business suit. He had a fat stomach that he held as he ran, as though he carried a balloon full of water. "Bobbie, where's the fire?" he said.

The hatcheck girl tapped the glass. "Take a look, Tops."

If Mr. Topper was surprised by what he saw, he didn't show it. His head went down, and his head came up again. Then he took another look, bobbing like a duck. He didn't seem sad, but he pulled out a handkerchief and touched it to his eyes. "Poor old Herm," he said. "Curtains, is it? Final exit; lights out." He dabbed his eyes again. "Still, the show goes on, doesn't it? I'd better take his name off the marquee. Alert the authorities."

As he turned to leave, Mr. Topper saw me at the top of the tank. This time he *did* show surprise. He put his hand to his heart, and his big stomach jiggled. "Holy cats, kid," he said, breathing hard. "What are you doing?"

I started to tell him, but he interrupted. He told me to get down, and he came over and pulled on my arm to help me. "What's your name?" he asked.

"Scooter King."

Bobbie snorted. "Ah, baloney! That's a made-up name."

"It's not," I said.

Mr. Topper jabbed me with a finger. "How long have you been here?"

"Not long." I wondered if he thought maybe *I* was the killer. "Honest. I just came in to see the Torture Tank."

"See anyone else?" he asked. "Anyone see you?"

"Yes," I said. "There was an old man in here. He came running out from behind the tank, like he'd been hiding there. He went out through the lobby. He knocked me down."

Mr. Topper grunted. "Kid, I don't understand a word you're saying. You'd better tell it to the police."

He went out to the lobby, leaving me alone with Bobbie the hatcheck girl. We just stared at the Torture Tank, through the glass at the body inside it. She chewed her gum for a while, then blew out a bubble that burst against her lips.

"Hello, Central! Give me no-man's-land," she said.

"What do you mean?" I asked.

She mocked me with a high, squeaky voice. "*Whadya mean? Whadya mean?* Ah, it's just something Herman used to say. It's a line from a dumb old song, from the war. Whenever anything went wrong, he'd look at you and say, 'Hello, Central! Give me no-man's-land.'"

I shrugged; I had nothing to say. Bobbie went back to chewing her gum. She was sure pretty standing there in her flimsy dress. She was a pash baby, all right.

"You know," she said, "Houdini's pretty lucky, when you think about it."

I started to ask "What do you—" but changed it. "Why do you say that?"

"Don't be a sap," she said. "What's the headline going to say? 'Man Found Dead in Torture Tank.' You know, Houdini has to pay thirty smackers a day to rent this crummy room so people can see his tank? Well, he just got his money back."

"You mean this will sell tickets?" I said.

"Like nobody's business." Bobbie smiled. "Houdini couldn't buy this kind of publicity for a million bucks."

It was the last we said before Mr. Topper returned. He brought a policeman, a man so big that he looked like a bear in a blue uniform. The cop wore a badge and carried a nightstick. He said his name was Sergeant Summer. He crouched down beside the Torture Tank and had a long look through the glass at the body of Herman Day. Or that was what he wanted us to think. It was pretty obvious that he was really staring at *us* in the reflections on the tank.

"Don't just stand there, fat man," he said suddenly, without turning around. "Go find everyone in the building. Bring 'em here, see."

"I beg your pardon. Are you addressing me?" asked Mr. Topper.

"I ain't talking to myself," said Sergeant Summer. "Now get going, see. If you need any help, take the skirt."

Mr. Topper didn't look happy about it, but he did what he was told. He and Bobbie went off through the lobby, and Sergeant Summer started pacing round the room.

"Sir?" I said.

"What?"

"Did Mr. Topper tell you about the old man?"

"The bird with a beard? Sure," said Sergeant Summer. "What about him, kid?"

"I followed someone down the bluff," I said. "A man with a long coat and a cane. He came from Viktor Valerian's house."

"The Russian spook?"

"Yes," I said. "I was there. I followed a man out of the house."

The policeman kept walking, circling the tank. "Who?"

"I don't know for sure, but I think—"

"He came in here, did he? You saw that?"

"Well, no," I said. "I kind of lost him."

The policeman stopped pacing. He looked at me. "So someone you don't know went somewhere you didn't see. Is that what you're telling me? Kid, you're a regular Sherlock Holmes."

I didn't like the policeman. He made me feel squirmy inside as he looked down at me. "There *was* an old man in here," I said. "I know that. He had a beard and a walking stick."

"So what?"

"So maybe he killed Herman Day," I said.

"Look, kid," said Sergeant Summer with a huge sigh. "Old men and murder—that's gin and soda, see. They don't go together." He made his hands into fists and knocked his knuckles together to show me how things couldn't go together. "You telling me an old man carried a body up there?"

He pointed with his fist. "Way up there, and heaved it into the tank?"

"Maybe Herman *fell* into the tank." I said. "Maybe he was leaning over and the old man hit him from behind with his stick."

"Why?"

"I don't know."

"You don't know nothing," said Sergeant Summer. "Now look, kid, murder's my business, see, and I don't need some punk like you sticking his nose in my business. So put a sock in it, kid. Sit down and shut up."

There was nowhere to sit except on the lid of the Torture Tank. I waited there until Mr. Topper and Bobbie came back. They brought two people: a man in a dressing gown, with a cigar in his mouth, and a dame with an hourglass for a body. She was older than Bobbie but a lot younger than Tops, and she was a knockout. She was a barbecue Jane.

Mr. Topper must have told them everything. They knew just where to look when they came into the room. The dame let out a squeal, then grabbed on to Mr. Topper's arm and pressed her face against his chest. "Oh, dahlin', it's awful," she said in a squeaky voice.

The man in the dressing gown smoked his cigar. He was the first person to look halfway sad at the sight of Herman Day. But he didn't say anything. He just looked at the Torture Tank and kept his hands in the pockets of his gown.

"You Melvin Knight?" asked Sergeant Summer.

The man nodded.

"Yeah, I thought I recognized your mug. I seen your act." The sergeant unbuttoned a pocket on his jacket. He pulled out a small black book and the stub of a pencil. "Okay, funny man, where you been the last couple of hours?"

"Asleep," said Melvin Knight. "In my dressing room."

"This time of day?"

Melvin shrugged. "I work late."

"When was the last time you seen Herman?"

"About eleven last night. When we came off the stage." Melvin took a puff on his cigar. The smoke that dribbled out through his nose reminded me of ectoplasm. "Look, Sergeant," he said. "Twenty years I've worked with Herman. I hated his guts, and everyone knew it. But open your eyes, pal. Do I look like a killer?"

He held out his arms and did a funny little pirouette with the cigar still in his mouth. Thin as a stick, older than Herman, he smelled of hair oil and soap. His wrinkles had wrinkles. He sure didn't look like a killer to me, but then he didn't look like a guy straight out of bed, either.

Mr. Topper still had the dame in his arms. He was stroking her gold hair with one hand. "If you ask me, I don't know why Melvin would kill his own partner," he said. "Knight without Day? That's bread without butter. That's Romeo without what's-her-name. Melvin's washed up now; he's finished."

"Hey, wait a minute," said Melvin Knight. For the first

time, he took the cigar from his mouth. "Hang on, Tops. What are you saying?"

Mr. Topper tried to smile, but it didn't work too well. "Sorry, Mel," he said. "But I gotta give you your pictures back."

"What?" said Melvin. He turned as red as the dame's lipstick. "You can't do this to me, Tops. Twenty years I've been carrying that no-talent bum. I finally get my chance to go it alone, and you're going to take it from me?"

"Hey, what can I say? A contract's a contract, Melvin."

"No. Don't say that. Come on," begged Melvin. "Not *this* week, Tops."

Sergeant Summer waded in. "What's so special about this week?"

It was Bobbie who answered. "Houdini's here."

"So what?"

"So it looks good if you're headlining with Houdini," she said. "You get a full house at every show. Big reviews."

"I see." Sergeant Summer made a note in his book.

Now the dame lifted her head. "Gosh, Mr. Topper," she said in her little-girl voice. "If Mr. Day is dead and Mr. Knight can't go on by himself, then who's going to be the headliner? Huh?"

"I guess that's you, kiddo," said Mr. Topper. "You can handle it, can't you, Kitty?"

"Gosh, I'll sure try my darnedest," she said. "Gee, thanks a bunch, Mr. Topper. I'm going to be the big cheese!"

Bobbie made a rude noise. "Yeah. What a lucky break."

She looked kind of sore, and she was shooting daggers at Tops and the dame. Sergeant Summer was writing like crazy in his little book. Melvin was puffing more smoke than the Chattanooga Choo Choo. And poor Herman Day just dangled upside down in the Torture Tank, ignored by everyone.

It seemed to me that Kitty wasn't the only one to get a lucky break 'cause Herman Day was dead. Melvin Knight was free of a partner he hated, ready to star on his own. Tops Topper had a barbecue Jane falling all over him, and I was sure *that* didn't happen every week. And Bobbie had to be thinking that this was her chance to stop checking hats and start acting onstage. The killer might have been any one of them, or the old man with the beard, or whoever had run down the stairs from the top of the bluff. It might have been Tom, Dick, or Harry—any of the thousands of people in the city. But I didn't think so.

I felt a little shiver inside me. I knew for a fact that I had met the killer, and I was sure we'd meet again.

4

FRIDAY, JUNE 4, 1926

FRESHMAN CHOKES ON GOLDFISH
RADIOVISION NEARS COMPLETION
WARNING COMES BY MAIL

Bobbie was right about the Torture Tank and Herman Day. The story was splashed all over the *Morning Herald*. Tops Topper made the front page, saying a bunch of crazy stuff about an old Burmese curse that he'd probably dreamed up in the night.

"I'll tell you this," he was quoted as saying. "I would never go inside that thing now. Not for all the tea in China. But Houdini's going to do it. He'll do it every night at nine-fifteen."

The Man in the Moon got into the act as well. "Ogle time at the Orpheum," the columnist called it. "Houdini's tank drawing big crowds. Even the flagpole sitter came down for a look. Now Tops Topper the talk of the town. Ding-dong! Is that wedding bells we hear for Tops and Kitty Moore?" There was a small picture of the manager and the actress making goo-goo eyes at each other.

I heard Bobbie's voice in my head: *He couldn't buy that kind of publicity for a million bucks.* She'd been talking about Houdini, but it seemed to me that Tops Topper had come out on top.

Mother pored over the news at breakfast. She loved sensational items. "Scooter, I don't understand it," she said. "You were part of all this. You were the one who found the body, for crying out loud. Why didn't you get your name in the paper?" She looked at me as though I was stupid. "You had your big chance, and you passed it up. You could have been an item in 'The Man in the Moon.'"

"I guess I was too busy," I said. "I was trying to figure out what happened."

"Well, it's a good thing you didn't end up with cement shoes or something. You've got too much imagination for your own good; that's your trouble." Mother smiled. "Even as a baby you were like that. You always loved little puzzles." She picked up her scissors and started clipping out the little items.

"Mom?" I asked. "Did you see the Stranger leaving the séance at Viktor's?"

"*Who?*" Her face wrinkled as she figured it out. "That Mr. Brown, you mean? J. Brown, with the wig and the sweaty hat?"

"Yes," I said.

"Well, not really," she said. "He was there one minute, gone the next. But I did see him come sneaking back."

That took me by surprise. "How long was he gone?"

"Oh, I don't know," she said.

"Did he have time to go downtown?"

"Scooter, I don't know when he *left*," said Mother, a bit impatiently. "I suppose he could have gone downtown; he had enough time for that. But he probably went to see a man about a dog, if you know what I mean." She stopped snipping and looked up at me. "Say, you're not suggesting he's the killer, are you?"

"I don't know," I said. "He might be."

"Well, you just keep out of it," said Mother. "It's not any of *our* business."

She went back to work with the scissors. For a while, the only sound was the snicking of the blades. But Mother didn't like long silences, and soon she started talking. "You know, you missed a good show," she said. "At Viktor's. It went on for nearly an hour after you left. There were spirit lights and wax impressions, and a telephone that talked to people."

She snipped out "The Man in the Moon." "It was like fireworks, Scooty: all this razzle-dazzle, a big flash, and then nothing. You sit and wait, wondering if it's over. There wasn't a sound—not a peep—for such a long time that we thought Viktor must have died in his cabinet. Then we heard this clanking, like ghostly chains, and something banging around in the cabinet. Finally, someone got brave enough to look inside. As a matter of fact, it was your Stranger. He got up and opened the cabinet door. Well, there was Viktor, still sitting in his chair, but shaking like a leaf. Now that's a showman for you. It made you almost believe in all his tricks."

"You think they were tricks?" I asked.

"Of course they were tricks."

"What about the blue light and the little piano?"

"Tricks."

"Then how did he do it?"

"Invisible thread." Mother kept snipping, the blades of her scissors flashing with light. "Maybe mirrors."

"I didn't see any mirrors," I said.

She added the clipping to the little pile beside her. "Look, Scooter," she said. "I don't know exactly how he did it, okay? But he *is* a fake; I could see right through him. He's good; I'll give him that. He's darned good. He gave the sort of show that I can see *you* putting on someday."

"Me?" I said.

"Well, sure," she said. "You're a natural. You'll take over from me when the time comes, won't you?"

I hadn't thought about it. Like most of my friends, I was planning to leave school when I turned fourteen. I just figured that I would go to work for Mother. It would be better than selling papers on the street or pedaling around the city handing out telegrams.

"Well, of course you'll take over," she said with a breathy laugh, as though anything else was ridiculous.

I watched her do the clippings. I wondered if she was right. When I got to be her age, would I be doing what she was doing now? Maybe we would have changed places by then, and she would sit, all wrinkled and gray, watching me work the scissors, muttering away about magic beans and money trees. It gave me the creeps to think of that. I wasn't so sure it was the future I wanted.

Suddenly, Mother looked up. "Scooter, get the door," she said. "I sense the mailman's coming."

An instant later, from the front of the house, came a knocking. It was the fast tap of "shave-and-a-haircut" that the mailman always used. If I hadn't been daydreaming, I would have "sensed" him myself. He wore enormous boots that shook the porch as he came up the steps.

I didn't like the mailman. He was too snoopy, too eager to get inside. He liked to gaze around the house as if he'd come to the dime museum to see the freaks.

When I opened the door, his face fell. He always grinned when Mother answered, and pouted when it was me. He held out the mail like a bunch of flowers, and he stared past me. "Tell Madam King there's only three things today," he said. "But one of them must be important. It's big as a book. Here."

He shoved it at me, hard and fast, so that I had to back away. Of course he followed, still holding the mail, and suddenly he was inside the house. He peered down the hall, probably hoping for a glimpse of Mother.

"Don't crumple that," he said. "Madam King will want to see it right away."

The way he was acting, he might have brought a stone tablet. But it was only the catalog from Bishop's Supply, heavy in its brown envelope. I pulled it from his fingers.

"Careful! There's letters too," he said. "A couple of letters."

"Okay. Thanks," I said, trying to push him back.

"There's one with no return address. No sender's name," said the mailman. "That's a big mystery, huh?"

"It sure is," I said.

"It's like it came straight from the spirits."

"Well, maybe it did."

He stared at me, wide-eyed. Then he seemed to wise up that he wasn't wanted. "Guess I'll be off," he said. "Anything outgoing?" He was always as eager to take *away* the mail as he was to bring it in. Today there was nothing, but he still went happily down the stairs, whistling "Everybody Loves My Baby." I took the mail to Mother, keeping the catalog for myself. As she read the letters, I opened the envelope and turned the pages, wishing she would buy a real séance table with hidden drawers and built-in rappers.

"Oh, look!" she said, holding up the first of her letters. "It's from Viktor Valerian. He's inviting me to his séance on Friday. Me and a guest. Isn't that interesting?"

"It's not surprising," I said. Mother was always getting invitations from men she'd met. She laughed at most of them and pretended they didn't mean anything. I knew she kept them all in a box in her bedroom. But the funny thing was, she never went out on a date.

"I found him rather charming," said Mother. "We only talked for a minute, though. On my way out, he kissed my hand."

I flipped through the catalog to the section on ectoplasm. The cheap stuff was just cheesecloth, but if someone coughed up enough dough, he could get ectoplasm that would take the shapes of hands or faces. I was trying to figure how it worked when Mother suddenly cried out in surprise.

"Goodness!" she said. "Oh, Scooter, what's this?"

Her hand was shaking as she passed me the card. Inside was a very short message.

The REGULARS are OUT!
YOU BETTER BE CAREFUL

"What does it mean?" I asked.

"I don't know."

"Who's it from?"

"It isn't signed! Look, there's no return address on the envelope." She shook it at me, then hurled it down on the table. "What's going on, Scooter? Who's watching me?"

The envelope landed face up. I saw it and felt cold. "Mom, nobody's watching *you*," I said. "Somebody's watching *me*." The envelope was addressed to Scooter King, Esq.

Mother looked and saw that I was right. "This is because of that murder, isn't it? You've got yourself tied up in that murder. It was the killer who sent you this."

"Who are the Regulars?" I asked.

"I don't know," said Mother. "They're probably with Al Capone."

"Mom, he's in Chicago."

"Well, like a branch or something. Men with tommy guns and molls. If they find you, they'll make you sing like a canary."

"Oh, Mom," I said.

"Don't laugh," she told me. "You should read *True Crimes*."

Mother picked up the envelope. She looked at both sides, then stood up and hugged me. "Oh, Scooter, maybe we should talk to the police."

"We can't," I said.

"Why not?"

" 'Cause they'll come and poke around." I was thinking of Sergeant Summer. I could picture him tramping through the house, opening drawers, peering into cabinets. In five minutes he would find the panel in the wardrobe; in ten he would know all our secrets.

Mother must have seen the same thing, because she let go of me and slowly slumped into her chair. "It would be the end, wouldn't it?" She touched the card with the tips of her fingers. "But we might have to do it anyway. I don't like to think of you in danger."

Neither did I. But I made like a hero and said there was nothing to worry about. "It's only a card," I said. "I don't think that killers send cards."

"So you think they're killers," she said.

I shrugged. The Regulars sounded scary, like a posse that was hunting me down. Part of me wanted to hide in the house, but Houdini was coming. He was going to do his escape from a straitjacket, and nothing could stop me from seeing *that*.

At one o'clock, I went downtown. I rode my bicycle as far as I could, until the streets were too crowded. Then I parked it by a lamppost at Seventh and Madison and went the rest of the way on foot.

Every man in the city, every farmer from every village, must have had the same idea. There were women here and there, but mostly it was men who packed the streets. At Delaware, even the trolley cars were blocked. I had to force my way through the crowd, going sideways and backward. There was such a roar of voices ahead that it sounded like a million bees.

The whole block outside the Orpheum was clogged from end to end. Even when the Great War had ended, the streets hadn't been so crowded. Now every window was jammed with faces, every inch of pavement covered. The men were standing so close together that the brims of their hats overlapped. There were people climbing lampposts, people clinging to power poles. And every single person of all the thousands there stood staring at a little figure

51

suspended high above the street. I squirmed to my left and looked up, and there he was!

I knew I would never forget that first glimpse of Harry Houdini. He was dangling from a beam that jutted out from a fifth-floor window of the *Herald* building. Upside down, suspended by his ankles, he writhed and twisted in the air. His legs were strapped and buckled together, and the rest of him was encased in the straitjacket, his arms wrapped round his chest. He looked like a maggot on a fishhook. And oh, how he squirmed! A row of buckles gleamed down his back, flashing sunlight. But no matter how he shook, it seemed he could never escape.

Then the crowd surged around me, and I couldn't see him anymore.

I made my way to the Orpheum, past the revolving door. I climbed up onto the window ledge beside it and braced myself in a corner.

Houdini shook and twitched; he wriggled and swayed. He looked like a man trying to shake away spiders or eels. Now and then the crowd grew quiet, and we could hear him above us. There was a popping and a squeal from the ropes at his ankles, a jingle of buckles, the desperate sound of his breathing. Then he bent himself double, reaching his head to his feet, and a great roar rose from all the people as he freed—with his teeth—one of the straps on his legs.

Soon he got another loose, and another after that, and he started working the straitjacket over his head. The long arms came last, and then he was free. The cheering and shouting were so loud that I had to cover my ears. Houdini, still upside down, swung the jacket like a lariat, then let it fall. It caught the wind and opened up, so it looked like a person tumbling down five stories. People surged toward it. Hands stretched up. I saw it land on a thousand reaching fingers and then vanish, sucked down into the crowd.

Five floors up, people in the *Herald* building began to bring in Houdini through the window.

The show was over, but not a person left. No one gave up an inch of space, but everyone pressed even closer as they waited for Houdini.

He came out through the front door of the *Herald* building. He was wearing a jacket and bow tie, with his white cuffs showing and his hair perfectly combed. For a moment he held up his arms in a V, and then he stepped forward into the throng of people.

I'd pictured him as huge. I'd thought he would tower above anyone there. But he disappeared among the crowd, sucked into it the way his straitjacket had gone. I could follow his movement only by the ripple of people as he came toward the Orpheum in a curving, twisting path. By luck he emerged right in front of me, stepping up from the street to the sidewalk. He was a short man, with a big head and graying hair. He looked powerful and fierce.

People were reaching out to touch him. They were pushing and shoving, stretching their arms over the shoulders of others. Houdini was being jostled to the left, away from the revolving door. He tried to move forward, but there were too many hands clutching his sleeves, grabbing his shoulders. He looked exhausted now, rumpled and sweaty. Bent forward, he struggled on without moving, like a man wading through quicksand.

I jumped down into the sea of people. "Mr. Houdini!" I shouted.

5

FRIDAY, JUNE 4, 1926

EXTRA!

HOUDINI EXTENDS INVITATION

I pounced right in front of Harry Houdini. With one hand, I held on to the door of the Orpheum. With the other, I reached out. "Mr. Houdini! Mr. Houdini!" I cried.

For a moment, it seemed that I'd scared him. He gave a little start, then grabbed my hand, and I pulled him in.

Round the revolving door we went, together in one compartment. We spilled out into the lobby, and Tops Topper himself came and kicked a wedge into the door, stopping it from turning as the crowd surged against it.

The roar was hushed. There was just the quiet of the theater, and Mr. Topper hovering nearby with his big belly shaking. Through the door at the end of the lobby, I could see the Burmese Torture Tank sparkling with light, all polished and clean. Houdini brushed his clothes; he straightened his cuffs. "I love a crowd, but sometimes it gets out of hand," he said. He was eyeing me closely. "Young man, I'd like to thank you."

"Don't mention it," I said.

"No, no. Really." He had a big forehead and narrow eyes of bright blue. The lines in his face made it seem that he spent most of his time being angry. But he smiled at me now, and that made me feel like his friend. He said, "Tops, could you—"

"Yes?" said Mr. Topper, springing forward.

"Could you leave a pair of tickets in this boy's name?"

"Certainly," said Mr. Topper. He tried to make it clear that he knew me. "Two for Scooter King?" he said. "Yes, sir."

Houdini didn't even look at Mr. Topper. "So you're Scooter, the boy who found the body in my Torture Tank? That must have given you a fright; I'm sorry. Now I hear you want to crack the case, is that right?"

I could tell that he was teasing me a little bit. He didn't really wait for an answer but gave me a friendly clap on the arm. "Well, you'd better start cracking," he said with a smile. "But first, I'd like you to be my guest tonight."

"Gee, thanks," I said. "That's swell, Mr. Houdini."

"Not Mr.," he said, laughing. "To you, it's Harry, understand?"

There wasn't a chance in a bazillion that I could call the man Harry. I had been reading about him since I was a little kid. I had seen him in the moving pictures. I had even sat yelling at the screen, warning him to "Look out!" for the automaton or to "Hurry, hurry!" as he wriggled in the Chair of Death, trying to escape its straps. Of course, there was no sound at the flicks, so I had never heard his voice. I was surprised, now, that it was nearly as high as a woman's. But even that didn't matter. Houdini was my hero.

"Come on," he said. "I'll let you out the back way. No sense in getting crushed."

We crossed the lobby. He held open one of the big doors, then followed me into the auditorium. I hadn't been in there since I was six years old, so it all seemed kind of new. I gazed around at the plush seats and the velvet on the walls, at the chandeliers above me. The sounds of our shoes echoed back and forth. When I talked, my own voice bounced back at me.

"How do you get out of that straitjacket, Mr. Houdini?" I asked. "Is it true you have to dislocate your shoulders?"

"Thank goodness, no," he said, with another laugh. "The trick is knowing how to loosen it. With enough practice, you could do it yourself."

"Oh, I don't think so, Mr. Houdini!" I said. "Not hanging upside down above the street!" My echo embarrassed me. It sounded like a squeaky mouse.

"Well, that's true; the height makes a difference," said Houdini. "Not many men can cope with heights as easily as me."

We went through a door and up some stairs, coming out at the side of the stage. I could see the backs of the huge curtains, drawn across the stage, and a wonderful tower of spotlights and ropes soaring up three stories through the space behind them. There were coils of rope and wires, a forest painted onto panels, a big, full moon that hung on wires above me. It was more than the bee's knees; it was wicked.

"Never been backstage, have you?" asked Houdini.

"No, sir," I said.

"Well, tonight, after the show, I'll bring you up," he said.

"Gosh! Really?" That was all I could say. I knew I sounded like a moron, but I couldn't help it.

Houdini took me through a workshop and a storage space, through the wardrobe room with its racks of clothes and hats and shoes. There was a row of wooden heads wearing wigs, some with beards, some with mustaches. We went down from there, to a long corridor with doors on every side. "These are the dressing rooms," he said.

I had never been happier. I was in a whole new world, and I felt like Professor Challenger making his way to the Lost Plateau. It was such a wonderful place that I wished I could be part of it.

"Why is there nobody here?" I asked.

"As a wild guess, I would say everyone's outside," said Houdini. "I understand there was some sort of performance going on a moment ago."

He made me blush, and again I felt stupid. But then he laughed his little laugh, and I knew he hadn't meant anything by it.

"When you come back tonight it will all be different," he said. "You'll see a beehive then, everyone hurrying around. You'll want to join my show; I can promise you that. When you see all the action, when you smell the lights and the sweat and the greasepaint, that's when it gets in your blood."

I thought it would be the cat's pajamas to be in his show, to go from city to city with Harry Houdini. I was trying to screw up the courage to tell him I'd like a job, when we came to the exit. Without pausing, he turned the handle and opened the door.

"Again, thank you," he said. "I'll see you tonight, Scooter."

Tongue-tied and embarrassed, I stepped outside, into a narrow entranceway. Nearly a whole block from the *Herald* building, a river of people was draining away from the big crowd. I wanted everyone to turn and look at me, to see me talking with Houdini. But they only went streaming past, and then the door closed behind me and I was alone.

I walked out of the entranceway, onto the sidewalk. I turned to my right and nearly bumped into Mr. Topper. He was leaning against the wall.

"Hello, Scooter," he said. "I was just catching a breath of fresh air." He lifted his nose and sniffed, as though smelling a bunch of flowers.

I started to walk around him, but he moved away from the wall, blocking my path. "By the way," he said. "I'm curious. Have you heard anything more about the murder?"

"Not really," I said.

"Did Houdini talk about it? Did he ask any questions?"

"Like what?" I asked.

"Oh, I don't know." Mr. Topper tried to smile, but he looked just terrible. "I was wondering if Harry suspected anybody in particular. Because, frankly, I'm in the dark here, Scooter."

"We didn't talk about it," I said. "There wasn't much time."

"I suppose not," he said. "So my name didn't come up? Nothing like that?"

"No, sir."

"I tried hard to get his name in the papers; I hope he appreciates that." Below the bulge of his stomach, Mr. Topper held his hands together. "He likes his name in the papers, you know. He's a publicity hound."

"Is he?"

"And then some!" said Mr. Topper, with a short laugh. "But I didn't tell you that. You understand?"

"Yes, sir."

Mr. Topper must have had something on his mind, but he didn't spell it out. He shuffled his feet, looking embarrassed, and then said suddenly, "Well, so long." Off he went toward the front of the theater.

Across the street and up the cliff stood the looming castle of Viktor Valerian. I thought I could see a shape in one of the narrow windows and wondered if it was the Russian looking down on the city. The stairs that brought me from his house started just to my left, and a few people were laboring up them, bent forward, in a line like mountain climbers.

I turned right, to start on my way home. There was a wind blowing between the buildings, and the garbage left by the crowd was swirling along the street. Sheets of newspaper went by like tumbleweeds. The wrapping from a Butterfinger bar whirled up in a yellow spiral.

Lying in the gutter was a clump of white hair. It looked at first like a dead rat, or like the tail of a cat that had been trampled by the crowd. I walked right past, not looking twice, until a tiny spark seemed to flash in my brain. Then I went back and took a closer look. The thing was gray and dirty, trodden by feet. I picked it up with the very tips of my fingers and tried to pull apart the strands of hair that were stuck in a gluey strip. I felt a small twinge when I saw what it really was: a man's wig, or maybe a false beard.

It was so dirty and scuffed that I couldn't tell the real color. Silver or white: it was hard to decide. But I didn't doubt that it had been dropped in the gutter by the old man who'd fled from the Orpheum—the old man who had killed Herman Day. Maybe he'd had the hair stuffed in his pocket; maybe he'd picked it up in the theater's wardrobe room. It didn't matter. All I had to do was take the clump to the police and . . .

I imagined Sergeant Summer laughing when he saw me with that dirty bit of hair dangling from my fingers. *I don't need some punk like you sticking his nose in my business.* So I threw the thing down and went along home.

When I got there, the door was locked. It took me

by surprise—and I crashed up against it, expecting it to open. My mother, sounding frightened, called from inside: "Who's there?"

"It's me," I said.

"Scooter?"

"Yes."

She opened the door, pulled me in, and slammed it shut again. "Oh, Scooty, I was worried," she said, looking out through the narrow window. "Someone came around while you were out."

"Who?"

"I don't know. A man. He said he wanted a reading, but I wouldn't open the door; I wouldn't even look out the window." She turned the lock and put the chain on its catch. "I wasn't taking any chances. I told him to come back later."

"We have to go out," I said.

Mother nodded. "That's a good idea."

"No, I mean we're going to the Orpheum," I said. She was heading for the living room, and I trailed behind her. "I got tickets to see Houdini."

"Really?" That made her happy. "Balcony or floor? Oh, what does it matter? I'm itching to see that horrible man."

"I met him," I said. "I talked to him, Mom."

"You don't say!" She sat down on the fainting couch. "Did he scratch you with his cloven hooves?"

"Mom, he's a nice guy. I liked him," I said. "He gave me the tickets. And you know what, Mom? I think I found a clue about the old man who knocked me over at the Orpheum."

"I don't want to hear about that," she said.

"But, Mom—"

"I don't want to hear!" she said, more loudly. She closed her eyes and clamped her hands on her ears. "I don't like you getting mixed up with murder. If you don't stop, you'll get yourself in real trouble."

6

FRIDAY, JUNE 4, 1926

EXTRA! EXTRA!

HOUDINI FACES DEATH

Mother drove the Stanley Steamer barefoot. She took off her high-heeled shoes and set them on the dashboard so that they wouldn't get scuffed by the pedals. She was wearing her raccoon coat, unbuttoned, because the ride home would be chilly. With her goggles and driving gloves, she looked like a big raccoon herself.

Stanley was nearly twenty years old. He'd been rattling around since before the Great War—before the *Titanic* went down, before Halley's Comet went shooting past. I hated the thought of pulling up to the Orpheum in that old breezer, so I made Mother park a block away.

When we got to the theater, people were streaming in from all sides. At the top of the big marquee, in black letters, it said, HOUDINI TONIGHT! Underneath, in smaller letters: *Kitty Moore*. There was no mention of Melvin Knight.

I felt pretty important going up to the ticket booth.

I shouted through the window: "Two for Scooter King! Houdini had them put aside."

We went through the door, into the lobby. Mother checked her coat at the counter, and it was Bobbie who took it. "Hi, Scooter," she said. "Nice to see you here."

Mother looked surprised, then amused. She whispered as we walked away, "My, you've been a busy boy."

Laughing to herself, she went to the powder room, leaving me to wander through the lobby. The fountain gurgled away, and the big Houdinis stared down from their posters. But the Torture Tank was gone from the separate room. Blocking the doorway was a wooden easel, and on the easel was a white placard. Across the top, someone had written, *A Challenge*.

I couldn't read the rest without going closer, so I pushed past a little boy with a teddy bear. He and the bear were both wearing sailor suits, and he let out a cry when the bear's little white hat fell on the carpet. I ignored him as I started reading.

> The people listed below practice as mediums in this city. They claim to have psychic powers. I challenge them to prove that the methods they use are legitimate. If they fail to meet my challenge, I will expose them as frauds.
>   —HARRY HOUDINI

The rest of the card was covered with names. There must have been more than a dozen—maybe twenty. Some I knew, and others were strange to me. There were Mr. McCordy, who did magnetic healing for young women, and Madeline Wick, who churned out pages of automatic writing that no one could read but herself. There was even Mrs. Snale, who was blind as a bat; she read tea leaves on Sundays for twenty-five cents.

But nowhere on the list was Viktor Valerian. And nowhere was Madam King.

Mother came up quietly behind me. Her high heels didn't make a sound on that thick red carpet. "Isn't this wonderful, Scooty?" she said, all bubbly with delight. "Did you put a penny in the fountain for luck? Come on, let's find our seats. Say, what are you looking at?"

I didn't even try to hide the challenge. I pointed with my thumb and watched as the expression of pride and pleasure fell from her face. I felt very sorry for her.

"Mom, you're not on the list," I said quickly.

"Yes, I see that."

Her tone surprised me. She sounded cold and angry.

"Well," she said. "Isn't this a slap in the face?" She put her hands on her hips. "Who does he think he is, that Harry Houdini? Has he never heard of Madam King? Or does he think I'm not worth the bother of exposing?"

"Mom, you didn't *want* him to come after you," I said. "You should be happy."

"I suppose that's true," she admitted. "Better to be a living dog than a dead lion, and all that jazz. It's just that I hate always being the dog, Scooter."

People were streaming through the big doors then, from the lobby to the auditorium. We joined the line, swept along down the aisle. Four rows from the front, we found our seats. Men turned to look as Mother squeezed down the row and settled into her place.

We were so close to the orchestra pit that I could see the violin players, and the men with the drums, and the top of the conductor's head as he bent over his music stand. The guy with the cello started playing, and soon all the others joined in. At first, it sounded as though they were playing different songs. Then the conductor tapped with his stick and waved his arms, and they all started up on the same tune.

People took their seats. The big curtain shimmered as someone brushed against it from behind. Then the lights went dim and spotlights came on, making a big circle on the red cloth.

Tops Topper came through the curtains like a cat through a cat door. He was wearing a black suit and a tall hat. When he raised one hand, the music stopped.

"Ladies and gentlemen," he said. "Tonight I bring you a new sensation. You will tell your children—you will tell your children's children—that you saw her at the Orpheum when she made her big debut. Please welcome Kitty Moore!"

He started clapping as he walked to the side of the stage. The music picked up again, and the curtain slid open.

All alone in a blue spotlight was the barbecue Jane. She wore long gloves that went up above her elbows, and a silver dress as tight as paint. It was made of spangles that flashed different colors whenever she moved.

Her golden hair was shining; her lips were shining. "Thanks a bunch," she said in her little-girl's voice. "This one's for you, Mr. Topper."

The music changed to a slow song, and she started to sing. Her voice was so soft that it barely rose above the violins. Even near the front, I couldn't hear what she was saying. But that didn't seem to matter to a lot of people. While the women sat back with their arms crossed, every man leaned forward. They put their hands on the seats in front of them, so they looked like row after row of dogs going on motorcar rides. Their tongues were nearly hanging out. The sparkles of light shooting back from the spangles on Kitty Moore's dress shimmered on their eyes and cheeks, in the lenses of the ones who wore glasses.

When Kitty Moore finished, when her whispery voice died away, the clapping rumbled like thunder through the auditorium.

She sang three songs. Then Houdini came out.

In his black jacket and bow tie, he looked tall and young to me now. He came to the edge of the stage, grabbed his cuffs, and ripped away his sleeves! They tore from his shoulders, jacket and shirt together, leaving his arms bare right up to the shoulders. Nobody was going to say Harry Houdini had anything up his sleeves.

He did magic tricks that were the eel's hips. Coins and cards appeared from thin air; metal rings floated like balloons; handkerchiefs knotted themselves together. He swallowed a ball of thread, then a hundred needles one by one, and coughed it all up again with the needles threaded in a perfect line that stretched right across the stage. He brought out his wife, a tiny, pretty woman he called Bess. He sealed her in a bag inside a box, raised a curtain, and somehow changed places with her in an instant. In the best trick of all, an assistant came out with a gun. He was a fancy Wally with slicked-down hair and he held up a bullet for all to see before he carefully loaded the gun. He stood on one side of the stage, with Houdini on the other. Then he spread his feet apart, raised the gun, and took careful aim at Houdini, steadying the gun with both hands. Slowly, he squeezed the trigger. There was a bang and a cloud of smoke. Houdini staggered backward.

From the audience came one huge gasp.

"Is he dead?" cried Mother hopefully.

I thought so. But Houdini straightened up and smiled, and there in his teeth was the bullet! He'd caught it in midair.

An intermission followed. When Houdini reappeared, he had changed into an evening coat with long tails that hung behind him like the feathers of a swallow. He stood again in the spotlights at the front of the stage.

"Ladies and gentlemen," he said. "I present to you the Burmese Torture Tank."

In the orchestra pit the drums began pounding. They

boomed through the auditorium and echoed from the balcony. They beat so loudly that I could feel the sound in my chest like a second heart.

Six men came out from the wings, pushing the enormous tank. There was no sign that Herman Day had died inside that thing, but everyone knew it. All over the theater, people stood up for a better look. The tank rumbled like a boxcar, flashing and glinting as the spotlights swept across it.

Houdini was here and there, darting about in his evening coat. The men set the tank on a huge square of red canvas. A massive hook lifted the lid from the top and set it on the stage, standing on its side. The music kept playing, the white gloves of the conductor and the violinists bobbing like rabbits over the edge of the pit.

Workers dragged a fire hose from the wings and began filling the tank with water. Houdini peeled off his coat, stripping down to the black trunks and vest of a bathing costume. He lay down on the stage so that his feet could be locked into clasps on the lid. His arms were handcuffed behind him. His body was wrapped in chains.

Above the gush of water, the clanking of locks, Houdini kept talking. He explained how he would be pinned upside down, under water, between the iron spikes of the Torture Tank. He said there would be a man standing by with an axe, whose only job was to smash the glass if it needed smashing.

Then he signaled that he was ready, and the hook hauled the lid into the air. Houdini rose with it until he was suspended upside down, twenty feet above the stage.

Ropes creaked in their pulleys. He hovered there above the Torture Tank. When water spilled from its top, the workers turned off the hose and dragged it away. Then Houdini tipped his head, and down he went, plunging into the water.

He vanished into a cloud of bubbles and foam. Water sloshed by the gallon from every side, and in the moment that he disappeared, I and my mother and everyone else drew a breath and held it.

Slowly, the water cleared. Houdini seemed to appear from a gray cloud, as though materializing in the tank. There he was, trapped among the spikes, cheeks bulging with his breath, hair floating like seaweed.

Workers slammed the bolts in place along the edges of the lid. They put on the locks and chains, sealing the tank like a fortress. A black screen was set up in front of the tank. The man with the axe stood beside it.

Already the first people in the audience were letting out the breaths they'd taken. My mother had held on for only a few seconds, but others squirmed in their seats, and some held their noses while their cheeks bulged like balloons. One by one, they all gave up, gasping breaths with sounds like small explosions. A minute had passed. Another went by. The last of the small explosions echoed in the quiet, followed by a wheezing gasp of breath. The third minute passed as we all gaped at the black screen.

At three and a half minutes, people began to mutter. At four, they were shouting. A man called out, "He must be drowning!" A lady leapt from her seat. "Save him!" she cried. "Break the glass!" But the man with the axe stood unmoved by the clamor.

Five minutes passed. Even my mother was fretting. I looked around and saw that everyone was as scared as I was. The shouting grew louder: "Help him!" "Save him!" Six minutes passed.

Houdini had been under water nearly ten minutes before the man with the axe leaned casually back and stole a look behind the screen. All at once, his mouth fell open, and he hurled himself toward the Torture Tank, swinging the axe above his shoulder. In his rush he toppled the black screen, and there—for all to see—was Houdini, bent horribly among the iron spikes, bashing white fists at the glass. His eyes seemed as big as baseballs.

The man grunted; his axe hurtled down. The glass front shattered, and the thousands of gallons of water gushed out, surging over the stage, tumbling into the pit in a creamy waterfall. Out leapt the conductor; out leapt the drummer. Ladies were screaming, and men were on their feet. Someone yelled for a doctor.

And the curtain came crashing down.

In a moment, the house lights were on, the ushers and

doormen trying to settle the crowd. They moved through the place like cowboys among a herd of cattle, muttering soothing words. But I sprang from my seat and ran to the stage, up the stairs that Houdini had shown me.

When I was halfway up I heard him shouting. I came out at the top to find him swinging in the air, locked in the lid of the torture tank, bellowing at the stagehands to bring him down faster. Water was pouring from his clothes, drenching tiny Bess, who stood right below him, reaching up to touch his hand. Mr. Topper had to move her away so that the men could settle the lid on the canvas square and unfasten Houdini's ankles.

Even half drowned, Houdini was strong. He was like a wet cat, struggling and furious. The moment he was free, he ran to the tank. "Give me a leg up!" he shouted.

"What are you doing?" said Mr. Topper.

Houdini pointed at a stagehand. "You! Come here!" He got the man to stand beside the tank and cup his hands to make a ladder. Then he climbed onto the fellow's shoulders and started prying and pushing at the locking mechanisms just inside the tank.

"Harry, please come down," said Mr. Topper.

Houdini didn't listen. He wrapped his hands around a clasp, pulling with all his strength. Veins pulsed in his neck; his arm muscles bulged.

"Harry, I insist," said Mr. Topper.

Houdini was turning redder by the moment. Then, with a small clicking sound, the clasp twisted in his hands, and a secret lock flew open. Onto the stage fell a small cylinder. Houdini pounced on it.

Out from the wings, in clattering heels, ran Kitty Moore. In her silvery dress, she had to move in little steps that made her wriggle like an eel. She went straight to Mr. Topper.

"Dahlin'!" she said, throwing her arms around him. "Oh, dahlin', what's wrong?"

Mr. Topper held her tightly. "There's been an accident. Houdini—"

She put her hand to her brow, as though she might faint. "Will I have to take over from him?"

"No, they saved him," said Mr. Topper.

Kitty cowered back as Houdini marched across the stage. He stopped only inches from Mr. Topper and held the tiny cylinder in the man's face. "See that?" he shouted. "Do you understand?"

I didn't have a clue what he was getting at. But Kitty Moore wasn't quite the dumb Dora that I thought she was, because *she* got wise to it right away. "Oh, dahlin'," she said, looking up at Mr. Topper. "Herman Day tried to murder Houdini. He tried to fix it so that Houdini couldn't get out of the tank."

"That's right!" said Houdini, half shouting. "He climbed up and jammed the lock. Probably reached too far and fell in. The fool! Bashed his own stupid head."

Houdini threw down the cylinder. It landed at the feet of Mr. Topper, who reared back like an elephant seeing a mouse. "Hey!" he said. "Why are you angry at *me*? It was Herman who did it."

"It's your fault!" cried Houdini. "Herman wouldn't have had the chance if not for you." He was so mad, he was spitting. "I knew it was a mistake to put the tank on display without a guard. I warned you this could happen."

Houdini turned and stalked away. When he saw me, he nodded curtly. "I'm sorry, but we can't talk now," he said, marching past. Bess—soaking wet—ran to his side and helped him off the stage. Mr. Topper and Kitty stared after them for a moment, then wandered away in the other direction.

The cylinder was left lying on the floor. I picked it up.

I thought it was just a bit of rolled-up cardboard. But I soon found out that it was a matchbook. On the cover was a green X formed by a pair of spotlights crossing, and three words printed in red.

7

FRIDAY, JUNE 4, 1926

EXTRA! EXTRA!

LATE-NIGHT VISITOR FRIGHTENS
MADAM KING

It was crazy how things could change. Herman Day turned from a murderee to a murderer, and everyone seemed pretty happy with that. They all said the same thing in different ways, but Bobbie said it best: "The rat caught himself in his own little rat trap."

I didn't know who called for Sergeant Summer. Maybe he was out in the audience all the time, sitting there in his blue hat with the badge at the front. But I didn't think so. I figured it was Kitty Moore, frightened of Houdini.

I was still holding the matchbook when the sergeant came striding up to the stage with a billy club swinging from his belt. He looked around and asked some questions but stayed only five minutes. He didn't even take the matchbook out of my hand when I showed it to him.

"So it's from the Limelight Club. So what?" he said. People were bustling around us, mopping up the water, sorting things away. "The Limelight's just another speakeasy, kid. Soon as we bust one, another opens down the street."

"But how do you know that this matchbook was Herman Day's?" I asked.

Sergeant Summer sighed. He bellowed at Tops Topper, clear across the stage, "Hey, fat man! Did Herman go to the Limelight Club?"

"Are you kidding? It was his home away from home," said Mr. Topper.

Sergeant Summer looked down at me. "Happy now? Look, kid, the case is closed, see. It's finished. It's wrapped up." His voice rose to a shout. "Now leave me alone, see. Do you understand?"

I could still hear him in my mind as we motored home a little later. Sitting high on the Steamer's seat, I thought I was maybe the only person in the world who figured things differently. For me, the case wasn't closed at all. But, then, I was the only one who'd seen the old man running from the Orpheum. No one else had seen the false hair thrown down on the street or the figure fleeing toward the stairs at Viktor Valerian's. No one else had gone through the Stranger's pockets and found a hatcheck stub from the Limelight Club. To me, it seemed likely that the Stranger was the one who'd jammed a lock on the torture tank.

The only problem was, it didn't make sense. Why would the Stranger want to kill Houdini? Why would he run down to the Orpheum and crack a guy on the head? And how did the Regulars fit into it? Was everything connected, or was I trying to force together things that didn't join up, just as Sergeant Summer had told me?

I was still thinking about it as Mother parked the old breezer in the alley. The headlights flared on our picket fence, making strange shadows on the house. Mother worked the throttle and the brake, trying to coax Stanley into his regular place.

"Mom, have you ever been to the Limelight Club?" I asked.

"What do you think?" she said, cranking the wheel around.

Obviously, she hadn't. Mother never went to a club more than once or twice a century. I had teased her one time by calling the Steamer her struggle buggy, and she had started crying, because no guy had gone driving with her since 1919. Men fell over themselves to ask her out, but she gave every one the brush-off. "I guess I'm waiting for Mr. Right," she liked to tell me.

"No, Scooter," she said. "I've never been to the Limelight."

"Do you know where it is?" I asked.

"Will you be quiet a minute?" she said. "This is hard enough."

Everywhere we parked, the Steamer dribbled a pool of water on the ground. It was like an old horse that kept wetting itself, and this spot was its bed. So the grass had turned to mud, and Stanley kept slipping sideways and backward. But Mother finally nudged him into place—or near enough.

The front end was angled up, the headlights shining into our apple tree. "There, that'll do," she said.

"So, Mom—"

She turned in her seat. "Now what's this all about, Scooter? Do you want me to take you to the Limelight Club? Is that what you're getting at?"

"Yes," I said, a bit surprised.

"You want to see if our Mr. Brown is there, I suppose."

I nodded.

"Then what, Scooter? If he *is* there, what will you do?"

I'd thought about it, so I answered right away. "Take his picture."

Mother laughed. "Take his picture? How is that supposed to help?"

"I'll give it to the police," I said. "They can show it around. Maybe someone saw him taking off his beard behind the Orpheum or running up the stairs to Viktor's house. At least they'll learn his real name, 'cause I doubt it's Mr. Brown."

Mother took off her driving gloves. She took off her goggles and shook her hair. "I don't know why you want to get more mixed up in this than you already are," she said. "Scooter, he was a harmless man."

"What if he's a Regular?" I asked.

"Oh, come on, Scooty." She was unwinding her long scarf. "He was just a nice man who lost his dog."

"I don't think so."

"Well, I don't know if we can find him at the Limelight

Club, or if they'll even let you in. But I'll try if you want. Goodness knows I won't have any peace if I don't."

"When can we go?" I asked.

"Oh, let me change and we'll go right now. All right?"

We got out of the car and walked toward the house. Mother was hurrying up the path, jingling her keys, when I saw the branches of the bushes moving.

It gave me such a fright that I nearly jumped out of my skin. I spotted a man sitting at the side of the steps, where a blueberry bush grew wildly over the railing. He was almost invisible against the branches, because his clothes were dark and his hat was pulled low.

Mother was just in front of me. I grabbed her coat and stopped her.

The man popped up. He had his hands in his coat pockets, making bulges in the cloth. He came down a step, then pulled out his right hand, and I thought I saw the barrel of a gun sticking out between his fingers.

"Mom!" I said.

The man raised the gun. But instead of pointing it at us, he wedged it into his mouth. Then he took his hand away, to tip up the front of his hat, and I saw that the gun was only a pipe. I felt kind of stupid about it.

Mother laughed in an odd way. "Dr. Wiseman!" she said. "Do you always surprise people in the dark?"

"Oh, I'm sorry," he said. "I hope I didn't startle you. I came by this afternoon—don't you remember?—and you told me to come back later. Well, here I am."

A sheepish look crossed Mother's face. So the man she had kept out of the house in fear of the Regulars was really Dr. Wiseman, the famous writer.

He took his pipe out of his mouth and put it back in his pocket. "I wanted so much to see you again," he said, pulling off his hat. "I haven't had you out of my mind since I met you at Viktor Valerian's."

"Oh, really?" said Mother. "How interesting."

I could almost hear her wheels turning. She was probably wondering if Dr. Wiseman had come to ask her to try out for the *Scientific American* prize. At that moment, she must have seen her money trees sprouting all over.

He held his hat in both hands, like a squirrel with a nut. "I know the hour's late," he said. "But would it be possible to have a sitting with you?" He glanced at me, then added pointedly, "A *private* sitting."

"Now?" said Mother. "We were on our way to—"

She caught herself in time. She wouldn't dare let on to Dr. Wiseman that we were going to a speakeasy. Everyone knew that he was a sworn teetotaler, a big booster for Prohibition.

He put his hand to his left ear. "Pardon me? You're on your way to where?"

"Bed," said Mother. "It's getting late."

"I only ask for a quarter hour," said Dr. Wiseman. "Please? I'll make it worth your while."

"Well, all right," said Mother.

We took him into the house. He wasn't very handsome, but he wasn't as old as the other fossils who came to the house. His hair was still dark, as unruly as a boy's. His eyes were blue, and they might have been stuck to my mother.

"We'll go into the séance room," she said, putting her long fingers on his arm. "I think we'll leave the lights dim, rather than have a dark sitting."

"Whatever you say," said Dr. Wiseman.

She gave me a look to make sure that I'd heard about the lights. Maybe she was worried that I would blunder out of the wardrobe with cheesecloth on my head. Or maybe she was worried that Dr. Wiseman meant to make it worth her while in kisses instead of money. At any rate, they slipped together into the séance room, and Mother closed the door.

I took a flashlight and went round to the kitchen, careful not to make a noise. I switched it off before I opened the panel in the back of the wardrobe. I crawled through and sat inside.

There was a funny thing about spiritualists. The more someone believed in table raps and spirit voices, the easier it was to put one over on him. A real believer could overlook nearly anything. So it took Mother only a moment to get started.

"I shall fall into a trance now," she said.

"No, wait!" cried Dr. Wiseman. I heard his chair moving. "Look, madam, I must be honest with you. I have come straight from Viktor's, where the *Scientific American* committee was meeting tonight without Houdini. The chairman and I have decided that we must finish the trials without him."

"Why?" asked Mother.

"The man's acidic!" said Dr. Wiseman. "He might even be dangerous. Houdini inhibits phenomena merely by his presence. There is no doubt that Viktor is a genuine medium. He is truly a miracle, Madam King. But the spirits never come through if Houdini is present."

"I'm not surprised," said Mother. "But why are you telling me this?"

The wardrobe was hot and musty. Through the hairline crack between the doors, I could see the glow of the gas lamps.

"It was Viktor's idea that I come to see you. I am merely the go-between," said Dr. Wiseman. "I thought it would be a delightful errand to bring the proposal to you in person."

"What sort of proposal?" asked Mother.

"It's a delicate matter," said Dr. Wiseman. "Please hear me out." He cleared his throat with a cough. "What we have in mind is this: you will accept Houdini's challenge."

"Me?" asked Mother.

"Yes, you, madam."

"You want *me* to challenge Houdini? To dare him to expose me?"

"Yes, Madam King."

"My," she said. "Oh, my, this *is* a surprise."

I put my eye to the crack in the door. I could see my

mother leaning back, her hand on her heart. She was more than flushed; she was *glowing*.

"Oh, Doctor." She flapped her hand in front of her face, fanning herself with her fingers. "Do you really think I'm that good? Can my powers stand up to Houdini?"

He didn't answer right away. He was so quiet that Mother said again, "Doctor?"

Dr. Wiseman spoke slowly and carefully. "Madam, you don't understand," he said. "We want you to fall on the sword."

"I beg your pardon?"

"For the cause. We ask that you sacrifice yourself," said the doctor.

"That's your proposal?"

"It is."

"I don't understand."

Dr. Wiseman was sitting forward, leaning one elbow on the table, his hand cupped to his left ear. "Madam, think what it would mean if we could lift the veil of death. The end of fear, of suffering. It would be the greatest discovery that man has ever made. The proof of immortality."

His voice was actually trembling. "Madam, it's been my life's work, and it's now within my grasp. We can give the world its first true medium, if only we remove Houdini from the trials. You can do that, Madam King. You can play a part in this great drama by distracting Houdini with a challenge."

"Why should I?" asked Mother.

"Because Houdini can't possibly pass up a challenge.

And because he can't be in two places at once," said Dr. Wiseman. "If we try to unseat Houdini from the committee, he will raise an unholy ruckus. But if we merely distract him, we can continue with our trials. A week from today, we will hold our last session with Viktor Valerian and award him the prize. While Houdini is busy with you, we—the committee—will advance the cause of spiritualism and give the world its guiding light."

"But what about me?" said Mother. "Wouldn't it be the end for me?"

"I'm afraid it would," said Dr. Wiseman. His chair shifted and creaked. "But look at it reasonably, Madam King. You're one of thousands—tens of thousands—across the country. Oh, you're infinitely better than Mrs. Snale, but you're still not in the same league as Viktor Valerian. Furthermore, you know you'll never reach his level. For the sake of spiritualism, we ask you to step aside."

"No!" said Mother.

"Will you think about it?"

"I will not."

"Would five thousand dollars change your mind?"

Apparently, it would—or might—because I heard the tiny sound of my mother drawing a breath. I couldn't imagine her passing up five thousand dollars, twice the value of the *Scientific American* prize. That was one big heap of dough.

"Ah, yes," said the doctor, "I thought it might."

"Why so much?" asked Mother.

"The truth is invaluable," said Dr. Wiseman. "Besides, I'll make it back in book sales."

I squinted between the doors at my mother. She looked pale, but she'd stopped fanning herself. "Do I have to decide right now?" she said.

"No," said the doctor. "I shall give you forty-eight hours. That is until the sixth of June. Please come to the Ritz and let me know your decision."

I heard him get up, but kept watching Mother. She looked up at him and asked in a sad voice, "Why did you choose *me*? You could have made the offer to anyone."

"No, my dear, we couldn't," said Dr. Wiseman. "Houdini has investigated every other medium in the city. Their names are on his challenge. For some reason, he seems to have overlooked you."

"So?"

"You must remain a mystery to him." Dr. Wiseman leaned closer to Mother. "Let's not forget that you're not without talents. Viktor thinks most highly of you. He says you have something of a reputation. He says you have what it takes."

"*Viktor* said that?" asked Mother.

"His very words."

I suspected the doctor was shooting a line, but Mother swallowed it. She agreed to consider the offer, and that was the end of the "sitting." When I met her in the hall, after the doctor had gone, I could see the marks of tears on her cheeks.

"I imagine you heard every word?" she asked.

I nodded.

"I've never been so humiliated," she said. "Dr. Wiseman comes to my house. Dr. *Stanford* Wiseman, the Spirit Doctor himself, has heard of me. But it's only because I'm such a hopeless cause!"

"He didn't say that," I said.

"But he meant it."

She reeled away, through the doors to the living room. "Oh, Scooter, I don't know what to do." She swooned onto the couch, the back of her hand on her forehead. "What a terrible choice. I love being a medium, but I want to be rich. For twelve years, I thought I could have it both ways. Now all of a sudden I have to choose: one or the other. I have to choose in forty-eight hours." She looked toward the clock on the wall. "Make that forty-seven hours and forty-nine minutes."

She rolled to her right, sprawled along the couch. "How would I spend the days if I quit? Needlepoint? I don't think so. Join a reading circle? Play mah-jongg? Oh, it sounds deadly!" She rolled to her left. "Then the nights; they'd be worse. I'd be twitching for a séance."

I tried to look interested, to really listen to her. But all I saw were dollar bills, five thousand dollar bills falling from the sky like green snowflakes, piling up on the ground. It was enough money that we could go to England. Not only could Mother tour her haunted castles, she could *buy* one. We could settle there, or travel on to Europe or Africa. Mother had always talked about Africa. I didn't see any reason why she shouldn't take the money. Unless . . .

"Mom?" I said. "Do you think Victor might really be on the level?"

"I don't know," she said. "I didn't *think* so, but who really knows?" She groaned to herself. "Oh, Scooty, it's too dreadful to lie here thinking about it. Let's go down to the Limelight right now."

"Sure, that would be swell," I said. "I'll get my Kodak."

We didn't talk on the way downtown. When we pulled up to the curb a block from the Orpheum, the time was eleven minutes past eleven. I thought it was a strange number. We walked toward the Limelight Club.

Mother didn't know exactly where the speakeasy was. We came to the Coconut Café, where a neon palm tree flashed brown and yellow in sizzling pulses. In its light I saw a door across the street, with a big green X painted in the middle. There was a man standing outside it who looked like a gangster's torpedo. He was flipping a coin in the dark, just flipping and catching. Whenever the palm tree flashed, that coin gleamed, so it seemed he was juggling sparks of light. A cigarette was hanging from his mouth, and the smoke swirled up to the brim of his brown fedora. His hand was the only part of him that moved. He kept flipping the coin and never looked toward us. He only spoke when we were right beside him.

"Whadya want?" he said.

"Is this the Limelight Club?" asked Mother.

"Maybe." He flicked the coin up. He caught it in his hand. "Who sent ya?"

"Nobody."

"Who ya lookin' for?"

I could see that Mother was ready to give up. She looked sad as we stood there in the dark, in the buzz of the neon tree. So I started whining like a little kid, trying to sound pathetic. "We're looking for my dad," I said. "We've been everywhere, mister. This is the last place in the whole city, so please, mister, can't you let us in? Please?"

He thought about it through two flips of a coin. He must have figured that I was going to start bawling, because he suddenly knocked on the door—with his heel, so that he didn't have to move. He didn't even drop the coin. He tapped once, then twice again, and in a moment the door opened.

I smelled cigarettes and cigars and gin. I heard a woman laughing, and a glass breaking, and a band playing swing pretty loud. "Gee, thanks, mister," I said, and we went in. Mother gave me a small smile.

The joint was packed. There were forty or fifty tables, more than a hundred chairs, but there were still more people than places. Lined up at a long bar were men in white suits, and flappers in cloche hats, laughing with their mouths open. On a stage at the back, the band was playing "Tiger Rag." The piano was hammering out a crazy string of notes, the trumpets were blasting, and people were bouncing round the little dance floor, all flinging their hands in the air, their fingers shaking, all shouting together, "Hold that tiger! Hold that tiger!" There were cigarette girls cruising between the tables with their little trays. People were shrieking, and people were laughing.

The smoke was a thick and stinky fog. It hurt my eyes as much as the blaring trumpets hurt my ears. But I loved the Limelight Club; I loved the razzle-dazzle. All together, it was the berries and then some.

Mother had to shout right into my ear. "This isn't a place for you, Scooty, so make it speedy. Do you see Mr. Brown?"

"No." I had expected to find the Stranger straight away, maybe to see him sitting by himself in a quiet corner. Now I realized that I might not find him at all.

Mother grabbed my arm and pulled me to a table where people were just leaving. We dropped into seats that were still warm. Seven glasses stood on the table around an ashtray heaped with ground-out cigarettes that were stained red on their ends from lipstick.

When the waiter came, I looked away. He was probably too busy to notice, but I didn't want him to see how young I was. He picked up the glasses and put them on his tray. Mother said something to him, and off he went, half running.

I wound the film through my Kodak, watching the numbers slide through the red porthole. Then I left Mother at the table and went away to search for the Stranger.

I had to jostle between the tables, dodging waiters and

cigarette girls. I headed for the dance floor, then cut over toward the bar.

Between the two, at the best table in the place, sat Kitty Moore and Tops Topper. They were both leaning forward, drinking one martini out of two short straws. Their noses were almost touching, and their eyes were locked together.

As I watched them, "Tiger Rag" ended. There was still a babble of voices, but the room seemed suddenly quiet. The dance floor began to empty. The trumpet players broke open their horns and shook out the spit, then walked down from the stage.

A lady got up in their place. In a black sheath of a dress, with long hair, she looked like a mermaid without a tail. Men wolf-whistled, and she smiled back. Behind her, the piano player started up. He was hidden by the open top of the piano, but I could see his legs, and they were too short to reach the pedals. They didn't even come close. I figured him for a boy not more than ten years old, but—like just about every man in the joint—he was smoking. Big balls of gray floated up like smoke signals.

This wasn't dancing music, so everyone settled in at their tables. There were four empty chairs around Mr. Topper's table, and into one of them fell a man and a woman all tangled together. The man was Melvin Knight, but it took me a sec to recognize the lady. I had seen her only once, in Houdini's show. She had vanished from a birdcage hung in midair, only to reappear from a giant radio cabinet, popping out to dance the Charleston. Now they cuddled and kissed as the singer vamped around the stage, belting out a torch song. The piano player's cigar smoke floated up into the haze above him.

I couldn't see the Stranger anywhere. But at the table beside Mr. Topper's, I spotted other people from Houdini's show. I saw the man who'd fired a gun to let Houdini catch a bullet, and Houdini's wife, Bess, the tiny woman who had stood soaking wet on the stage reaching up to the half-drowned magician.

It hit me that any one of these people could have picked up a matchbook from the Limelight Club and used it to jam the lock on the Torture Tank. Herman Day might have caught the person in the act, tried to interfere, and got himself killed for his trouble. The fact was that I didn't know what had happened. Lurking around in a speakeasy sure wasn't going to help me find out. If I really wanted to uncover the killer, I had to flush him out.

I lost myself in thought. The lady stopped singing, but I didn't know it. Suddenly, the stage was empty, and I was standing there like a palooka, staring at a bunch of people that maybe included a killer. I went back to the table.

But Mother wasn't alone.

8

FRIDAY, JUNE 4, 1926

EXTRA! EXTRA!

PIANO PLAYER COMES UP SHORT

In the chair that I'd left sat the piano player. I knew him by the puffs from his cigar and by the tiny black shoes that swung in midair, high above the floor, as he drummed his heels on a table leg.

But he wasn't a boy at all.

He was a dwarf, with the yellow teeth of a horse. His vest was smeared with the gray ash from his cigars. His voice was loud enough that I heard him from halfway across the room.

"What do you say, toots?" he said. "Why's a classy dame like you sitting here alone?"

"I'm *not* alone," said Mother.

"Could have fooled me." He laughed, letting out a greasy gush of smoke. "I don't see anyone else sitting here."

"In a minute you will," said Mother. She was as nice to him as she would have been to anyone else. But all I saw was a horrible man making like Rumplestiltskin.

"So, who you waiting for, toots?" he said. "How about you and me, we wait outside?"

I reached the table then. The dwarf glared as I slid into another chair. He puffed smoke in my face. "Beat it, kid."

"Don't tell him that," said Mother. "This is Scooter. He's my son."

The dwarf looked from me to her and back again. "Kind of young to be in a joint like this, aren't you?"

I shrugged.

"Where's your daddy at?"

"I don't know."

He barked a mean laugh, snorting smoke through his nose. "You don't know where your daddy's at?"

All around was the sound of laughing, of glasses clinking, of people being happy. But the only thing I heard was the mocking tone of that dwarf. "Gee, that must be some daddy you got. You going round to every speakeasy and blind pig, trying to run him down? Is that what you're doing?" His big teeth showed as he smiled. "Yeah, that must be some fine daddy."

"He went missing in the war," said Mother flatly. "We don't know if he's alive or dead."

It was a lie, but she made it sound like the truth. It slapped the dwarf's horrible smile from his face. "Oh, gee, that's too bad," he said. He stood up on his chair and leaned across the table. Between his fingers, the cigar shed ashes on the red tablecloth. "What was the guy's name, toots?"

"Joey," she said. It was another lie. "But you know what

96

everybody called him? Fat Daddy. That's right. They called him Fat Daddy, not because he was fat, but because he was just the sort of guy you'd call Fat Daddy."

The dwarf swallowed her line. "Yeah, I can picture him, toots," he said. "I think I might have met him."

"It's possible," said Mother. "He played the drums, didn't he, Scooter? He played with Jelly Roll Morton."

I nodded.

"We keep looking for him; what else can we do?" she said. "Wherever jazz is played, we hope to find Fat Daddy."

"I'll watch for him," said the dwarf. "If I ever meet a guy called Fat Daddy, I'll tell him Scooter's looking for him. Is that right?"

"Yes," said Mother. "Thank you."

He swung himself down from his chair. Standing up, he wasn't much higher than the table. His eyes were about level with the top as he stared across it toward the door. "See who's coming in?" he said.

We turned to look. It was Harry Houdini, pausing at the entrance, scanning the room.

"Poor schmuck," said the dwarf. "He comes in nearly every night looking for Bess, his wife. He never drinks a drop, hardly ever stays more than a minute. Just comes in and drags her out."

Houdini headed for the table beside the dance floor.

"He's going to be dead, you know," said the dwarf. "That's the rumor. Dead within the year." He winked at my mother. "Maybe sooner, huh?"

Houdini was already leaving again, and little Bess was with him. They went hand in hand, like newlyweds.

"So long, Mr. Big Shot," said the dwarf. He waved his tiny hand at Houdini's back. On the tips of his fingers were black dots, the marks of old burns that I figured he'd got from tapping his cigar. He took a puff, blew out the smoke. "Well, I'll see you, toots," he said.

With that, he was gone. He went away rolling like a sailor, with his cigar trailing smoke behind him. I had a funny feeling that I had already met him, though it seemed impossible. I couldn't remember anyone like him ever coming to one of Mother's séances. Still, the feeling left me with a prickling coldness on my arms.

The music started again. The dancers flocked back to the floor. Mother sat moving to the music: rocking in her chair, bobbing her head. But half an hour later she said she had a headache. She wanted to go home.

The Stranger hadn't arrived. No silver-haired man had come through the door. So I left with Mother, and that night—at home—I did something I hadn't done for a long time. On my way to bed, when I said good night to Mother, I asked about my father.

"Pop was never in the war, was he?" I said.

"No," said Mother. She was sitting on the fainting couch, rubbing her feet. Her high-heeled shoes—now on the floor—had left red welts on her toes.

"Did he ever play in any bands?"

She smiled. "Scooter, he couldn't carry a tune in a bucket."

"Then why did you give that guy the double talk tonight?" I asked.

"Because he was a real flat tire. And because I didn't want to tell him the truth." Mother winced as she pressed at a sore spot. "In case you don't already know, I'm not too proud of your father."

Pop went away when I was six years old—on a Wednesday, if what Mother had told me was true. I didn't remember the day of the week, but I sure remembered that night. Between dinner and dessert, Pop had got up from the table. "I think I'll stretch my legs," he'd said. I had asked to go with him, but he wouldn't take me. He went out, and I never saw him again.

I couldn't remember much about him. He'd had a beard, but only sometimes. Only when it was cold. I could picture him smiling, but no more than that, as though his whole face was a happy row of teeth. Often, he had lifted me up—to show me candles on a Christmas tree, or a passing parade, or a rainbow in the sky—or to let me ride on his shoulders, until I pulled too hard on his hair. I remembered that he had a smell, but I couldn't remember the smell itself. But once in a while I would smell it, and then—for a moment—I could remember.

Of course there were other kids around who didn't have a dad, on account of the war and the flu and everything. But

I thought mine was the only one who had gone out to stretch his legs and simply disappeared.

"His legs must be pretty long by now," I said.

Mother didn't answer. I was hoping she would laugh, but she didn't.

"Why don't we have any pictures of him?" I said.

"I threw them out," said Mother, kneading her toes. "It was silly, and I'm sorry. I should have kept them."

"I think he's dead," I told her.

"Well, I'm afraid you're wrong."

"How do you know?"

She looked up at me then. When she spoke, she sounded sad and tired. "Scooter, do you believe in me at all?"

"Mom," I said, "I—"

"No," she interrupted. "If your father was dead, I would know it. I would see him, or speak to him, or hear about him. Somehow, I would know, because I'm in touch with the spirit world. And if you don't believe that, you tell me right now."

I wished I had never started this. I stared back at her, wondering what to say.

"I see," she said, nodding. "First Dr. Wiseman, and now you. Is that it? Well, isn't this the perfect end of a wonderful day?" She collected her shoes and stood up. "Thank you, Scooter."

"Mom . . ."

"No, I mean it. Thank you," she said. "I was wondering

what to tell Dr. Wiseman. You've helped me make up my mind."

For the first time in many months, we didn't say good night to each other. Mother brushed past me, and the breeze from her clothes was chilling. She went upstairs to her room.

In the morning, when I heard her bustling around in the kitchen, I was almost scared to go down and see her. I didn't want to start again on the same subject. But I didn't want to sit in a chilly silence either. So I went down whistling, as though nothing had happened.

The Saturday *Herald* was on the table. But it was still rolled up in a tube, the way the newspaper boy had delivered it.

"Aren't you going to read the paper?" I asked.

"Not today." She was making coffee on the stove. The percolator was just beginning to boil.

"Can I read it?" I said.

"Be my guest."

I felt uncomfortable—creepy inside. But I tried to be funny. Sitting back dramatically, I crossed my legs and snapped open the front page.

HOUDINI DEFIES DEATH

The letters were three inches high, the headline bigger than the story. The reporter described how Houdini had failed to escape from his Torture Tank. There was a bunch of quotes from people in the audience, though they sounded like things the reporter had made up himself. There was no mention of the matchbook. There was nothing about Herman Day. But at the very bottom was a quote from Tops Topper: "Is there no doubt now that tank is cursed? I can't imagine how any man could be brave enough to get back inside it, not after what I have seen. But Houdini will do just that tonight. The Torture Tank has been repaired. Harry Houdini will return to the stage to face death in the face at nine-fifteen."

I turned to "The Man in the Moon." He started his column with the Torture Tank: *Even Houdini can't escape the rumors: was that a setup on the stage last night? Tops Topper plays tight-lipped, but tipsters say Tops planned it all.*

On the stove, the percolator was boiling hard. The glass knob bubbled, and the pot rattled on the burner. Mother stayed right there until the bubbling stopped, while the kitchen filled with the smell of coffee. She poured a cup and brought it to the table.

"Well, in case you're interested, it's over," she said.

I looked up. "What's over, Mom?"

"What do you think?" She sounded sore that I didn't know what she was talking about. "The whole thing. The whole deal. Scooter, I'm quitting."

It was as though a spirit had touched me; I felt a shiver down my back.

"Viktor's a phony. But I don't care; I'm still taking the

money," she said. "I thought about it all night. I decided that if I turn down that five thousand dollars, I'm out of my mind. You might as well put me in the bughouse right now if I do that, because I've got wheels loose in my head."

I pushed the newspaper aside. "Mom, is this because of what I said last night?"

"That was part of it, yes," she said. "You made me see that I'll never get famous and rich on my own. I just don't have it, do I? I'm not Viktor Valerian."

I could see she was disappointed. "I'm sorry," I said.

"Oh, don't be sorry." She glanced at the paper, at the big headline. "I wanted to be a medium so that I could help people. I wanted to give comfort and advice. But if no one believes in my powers—not even my own son—I don't know why I should bother."

I felt rotten inside. I wanted her to take the money, but I didn't want to be the reason that she quit. "Mom, remember what you said about the *Titanic*? About everything changing, and people making themselves rich?" I asked. "Well, you did that, Mom. You made yourself into a medium."

"A *failed* medium." Mother took a drink of her coffee. "Do you know what I'll miss the most? Speaking with Dorothy, I think. Oh, I know she's not real, but she's sort of real. I just love talking to Dorothy. I'll miss that, and I'll miss the people coming by in the night, sitting in the dark around the table, everyone nervous and edgy. I'll miss it like mad." She held her cup in both hands, looking at me over its edge. "Now, don't worry. I know you want me to take the money, and I will. My mind's made up. I'm going to go see Dr. Wiseman this morning."

She took another drink of coffee. Then, just like normal, she read "The Man in the Moon." Halfway through, we heard someone tramping up the front steps. "Mailman," said Mother.

But it wasn't the mailman at all. I went to the door to find an old lady in enormous shoes, deaf as a post, looking off across the garden. She didn't hear me when I said hello. So I reached out and touched her shoulder, and her teeth actually fell from her mouth. I watched them bounce across the porch.

The old lady picked them up. She shoved them into place, then gnashed her jaws together.

She smelled like peppermint with a dash of mothballs. Her clothes were black, and her hat had a little veil built into the front, just long enough to cover her nose with its thin mesh. She was holding two things in her hands: a long hearing trumpet and a bit of paper. I brought her into the house, guiding her through the door.

I thought Mother's money tree had sprouted.

9

SATURDAY, JUNE 5, 1926

TEDDY ROOSEVELT GETS HEAD EXAMINED
IRVING BERLIN MARRIES HEIRESS
WOMAN SEEKS PRIVATE SITTING

The piece of paper in the old lady's hand was a yellow card. One of Mother's magic beans had come home, and in a moment we would know if it would sprout a money tree or not.

I led the old woman into the vestibule and got her seated in the wicker chair.

She took off her little hat and held it in her lap. Her hair was the color of mushrooms. She gave me the yellow card.

I knew the message by heart; it was no different from any other. But I pretended to read it again, then put it carefully in my pocket. "So you've come for Madam King," I said.

She put the end of the hearing trumpet in her right ear and aimed the bell toward me. "Pardon me?" she said in a shaky voice, leaning forward in the chair.

I had to bend down and shout right into the mouth of the trumpet. "You're here for Madam King!"

"Yes," she said. "Is she in?"

"The madam is waiting!" I shouted. "She's expecting you!"

It lost some of its effect, to tell her this at the top of my voice. It lost even more when I had to repeat it twice. Most people were very impressed when they arrived out of the blue, to be told the madam was already waiting. But the old lady just sat and stared while her mouth moved as though she was chewing on a poppy seed.

I opened the drawer in the spindly table. I brought out the pen and a sheet of paper and told the old lady to write down a question. "Address it to a spirit!" I yelled. "To anyone you please!" From the same drawer I got the box of matches. I lit the candle that stood on the tabletop, and dropped the burnt match into the turtle-shaped ashtray.

When I looked again, the old lady was just sitting there. The hearing trumpet was in her hand, the sheet of paper in her lap, balanced on top of her hat. She looked at me helplessly.

"Oh, I'm sorry," I shouted. "You need something to write on!"

I looked around the tiny room, then took a book from the pile on the table. It was the new mystery by Van Dine, its paper jacket still crisp and clean. I placed it carefully on the knobs of the old lady's knees, taking her hat out of the way. I even helped her position the writing paper on the back of the book.

She frowned. "What shall I ask?"

"Anything you like!" I bellowed into the trumpet. "I'll tell the madam you're here."

I was surprised to find Mother still in the kitchen. She was reading the *Herald* as though she had all the time in the world.

"Why aren't you getting ready?" I asked.

She licked a finger, turned a page of the newspaper. "Ready for what, Scooter?"

"Your sitting!" I said, frustrated. "Mom, it's a yellow card."

I put it down on the table, right on top of the paper. Mother didn't touch it; she barely looked. In the flattest voice I'd ever heard, she said, "My, isn't that interesting." Then she turned another page.

I snatched the card. I read the coded number on the back. "Jeepers!" I cried.

Mother ignored me.

"Look!" I waved the card under her nose. "It's one of those three we sent out just the other day." I couldn't remember a yellow card ever coming back so quickly.

"Scooter, I don't care," she said, holding up her hands. "I'm finished; I'm done; I'm not a medium anymore."

I opened the file in the sideboard. I took out the clipping—the death notice—that matched the number I'd written on the yellow paper. "Mrs. Edith Mars," I said.

Mother said nothing.

I went to the rolltop desk and pulled out a box of clippings. There were two filed under "Mars": a note about Franklin Mars singing in the choir at a Christmas pageant, and an old clipping from "The Man in the Moon," now yellow and crisp. I read that one aloud. " 'Will Edith Crocker be the first woman on Mars? Fetching widow finds the eye of wealthy bachelor Franklin J. Mars. . . .'

"She must be loaded," I said.

Mother pretended not to care, but I could tell that she was intrigued. Her head turned very slightly, as though to hear me better. I read out the important parts of the obituary. "Her husband's name was Franklin. He died in a motorcar accident. Oh, wait, that was her *second* husband. The first one—Peter Crocker—died on the *Titanic*."

"Really?" Mother's cup rattled on its saucer. "The *Titanic*?" she said.

"That's what it says."

Mother could never resist the *Titanic*. "Well, maybe I should do one more sitting," she said. "Just one more, and that's it."

She turned around in her chair. She closed her eyes as I filled her in from the obituary. "Franklin had four children," I said. "Freddy was killed in the war. Jeremiah died in a flying accident. Kermit is still living, in Seattle. The only daughter, Jane, died of—"

"Slow down!" said Mother. She was trying to remember it all. "What was the name of the first husband? Who fathered the children?"

I sorted out the names and dates. It was one of Mother's talents that she could remember long lists and never mix them up. When she had the names straight, she nodded.

"I'll go and get dressed," she said. "Give me a moment, then bring Mrs. Mars to the séance room."

"She's deaf as a post."

Mother was already in the doorway. She spoke without stopping. "Oh, that's always fun."

I saw her running up the stairs as I went back to the vestibule. Mrs. Mars was sitting perfectly still in the wicker chair, with the book on her lap, the sheet of paper on top.

"Have you written your question?" I shouted.

She put her hearing trumpet in place. I shouted again, and she answered, "Yes, I have." She held up the paper.

"No, don't let me see it!" I turned my head away, shielding my eyes as if even a glimpse of the note might strike me blind.

"Goodness, I'm sorry!" squeaked Mrs. Mars.

"Fold it three times, please. Into a strip," I shouted.

I stared at the candle as I waited. Three beads of wax went dribbling from the top before old Mrs. Mars called out that she was done. I took the paper and touched it straight-away to the candle flame. There was a burst of strange light—of yellows and reds—because I'd treated the paper with phosphorous. It burned away in a flash, leaving nothing but shriveled ashes that I dropped into the ashtray. The old lady had seen it go straight from her hand to the candle flame, and she looked perfectly shocked.

"You didn't even read it!" she said.

"It wasn't meant for *my* eyes, ma'am," I told her. "It was between you and the spirits."

I heard my mother thundering down the stairs. I held out my hand to Mrs. Mars. "Please come with me."

The old lady tottered beside me. I had to walk so slowly that I felt like a pallbearer. We went down the hall, into the séance room.

Mother had pushed the table close to the wardrobe. In her chair, she had her head lowered.

"Madam King?" I said.

She lifted her head. "Ah, Mrs. Mars," she said.

The old lady hadn't given her name. She looked amazed to hear it, as though she'd witnessed a miracle.

I got the old bat into her seat, adjusted the shutters and curtains, turned down the gaslights, and closed the door on my way out. As soon as the latch clicked, I ran to the vestibule. I snatched up the book, tore away the dust jacket.

Inside, taped to its back, was a carbon. Under that was another sheet of paper, with the old lady's message to the spirits copied perfectly in black:

Dearest Franklin,
Please give me a sign that you are now in Summerland. Is it how we thought it would be? Is Millie there with you?
Love, Edith

I took the paper, and the old lady's purse, to the kitchen. I grabbed a pencil as I made my way into the wardrobe, not worrying too much if I made any noise. Kneeling inside, I opened the purse and shook it out.

What a sad little pile of things landed on the wardrobe floor. There were a few peppermints, a postage stamp, a receipt for the black hat she was wearing. There was a box of liver pills, and a wallet so old that the leather was cracked, the threads coming loose. It was the most tattered wallet I'd ever seen, but it had eighty-five dollars inside it, more money than I'd ever held at once. There was a photograph of a man with his hair parted in the middle, a monocle stuck in his right eye, its thin chain looped around his neck. On the back of the picture, someone had written, *Franklin, November 1919.*

I could hear Mother getting ready. She shouted at Mrs. Mars. "I will fall into a trance now."

I waited as she hummed and moaned. When the wailing started, I folded the sheet of paper with the question written on it and slipped it through the gap between the wardrobe doors. I wiggled it up and down, close to the floor, where it would be hidden by Mother's chair. In a moment, I felt it being pulled away.

Next, I passed Mother the photograph. Both came back a minute later, wriggling through the slot. Then Mother started shouting in her trance voice. "I call on the spirits!" she yelled. "I ask them to join us! If you can hear me, give me a sign! Knock once for yes, twice for no! Can you hear me?"

I tapped my pencil loudly on the wardrobe's floor.

"Oooh!" cried Mrs. Mars.

"There is a man trying to speak!" shouted my mother. "He is trying very hard to talk through me. He has a message to deliver, to a lady named Mary."

"Yes, that's me!" said Mrs. Mars.

"I believe his name is Frank. No, it is Franklin!" shouted Mother. "He is having trouble speaking, for he has only recently arrived in Summerland."

My mother groaned and muttered. "He tells Mary that he is happy. He wants her to know about his spectacles— no!—it's a monocle! He is saying that he has no need of it now, that his vision is perfect. He is young again! But he still wears the monocle out of habit. It hangs from a gold chain round his neck."

"Yes, he's had that for years," said Mary Mars. "Oh, thank goodness." She raised her voice, screeching into the shadows. "Franklin, can you hear me?"

I tapped once with the pencil.

"Are you alone?"

I tapped twice.

"No, not at all," said Mother. "He has constant companions. On Fridays he sings in the same choir as Donizetti and Puccini. Just now he sits with the spirits of two other men. One is named Freddy, the other Jeremiah. There is also a young woman called Jane."

"His children!" said Mrs. Mars. "But Jane was a child. She was only two when she died."

"She has grown up in Summerland," said Mother. "She is now a beautiful young woman."

"Well, fancy that," said Mrs. Mars happily. "Is there anyone else?"

I tapped once with the pencil.

"Yes. There is a gathering of men and women—it is like a club—and in the center is Captain Smith of the great ship *Titanic*. It includes John Jacob Astor and Mr. Charles Hays and—oh, there are too many to name. But among them is a man called Peter—Peter Crocker—"

"Is that *my* Peter?" asked Mrs. Mars.

I tapped once.

"Yes, it is," shouted Mother. "Franklin has come to know Peter, and the two are now friends. Franklin has been drawn into this circle through his friendship. He likes to hear stories of how the big ship—"

"Who else is there?" Mrs. Mars sounded worried. "Do you see anyone else?"

I tapped once. Mother said, "Yes, I see a woman. Her name begins with an M. It is like *Miller*."

"Millie?"

"Yes, that's it," said Mother. "She is there with Peter now, and she is very young and beautiful. And . . . oh, my."

Mother sounded strange. I tried squinting between the doors, but I couldn't see anything except the back of her chair.

"Now Franklin sees Millie," said Mother, "and—"

The old woman shrieked. "You hussy!"

"She doesn't want him there," said Mother.

But the old lady kept shouting. "Get away from him, you shameless tart."

"Everything's fading," said Mother. "I can't keep contact."

"You keep away from him!" cried Mrs. Mars.

Through the wardrobe doors, I heard a bang and a thud. Mother said sharply, "Please stay in your seat!"

"I knew she would do this!" said Mrs. Mars.

My mother brought the sitting to a sudden close. I had to hurry to get everything stuffed into the purse, to get the purse back where it belonged in the vestibule. I ran through the house, then back to the séance room. When I opened the doors, I saw the old woman on her feet, and my mother hugging her with both arms. The hearing trumpet was lying on the floor, and Mrs. Mars was shaking. "I was afraid this would happen," she said. "This is my biggest fear."

"Please don't worry," said Mother.

The old woman was talking in a pathetic, quiet voice. "Before I came along, Mildred and Franklin were an item. I knew—I just *knew*—that she carried a torch for Franklin. Even death wouldn't stop her."

"There, there," said Mother, patting the woman's back.

"I always dreaded that Franklin would go before me." Mrs. Mars had tears dribbling down the many cracks in her face. "I just knew that hussy would be waiting for him."

It was a horrible thing to see an old lady so sad. My mother kept patting her shoulders.

"What if I'm alone forever?" said Mrs. Mars. "Forever

and ever and ever, while that dreadful Mildred has my husband?"

"Please listen," said Mother. "You won't be alone; he's waiting for you!" Her cheek was touching the old woman's hair. "Oh, Scooty, please bring me her trumpet."

I picked it up from the floor. The metal was tarnished by age, except in the middle, where the old lady's fingers had made it more shiny than silver. I put the narrow tip against her ear and held the trumpet while Mother bellowed into its mouth.

"Your husband adores you. I could feel his love," she said.

"You did?"

"Oh, yes, it was powerful."

Mother kept talking. It took her five minutes to soothe the old woman, to get her quiet and happy again. Then all three of us went down the hall to the vestibule. Mrs. Mars, still sniffling, opened her purse and gave Mother a twenty-dollar bill.

That was more than anyone had ever offered. Mother gasped when she saw it. "Oh, no," she said. "This is too much."

"Nonsense!" Mrs. Mars opened her purse again and took out *another* twenty! "Bless you," she said. "You've got a great gift, Madam King."

She put on her coat and hat; she hooked her handbag over her arm. Small and bent, but looking brave as a lion, she went out the door and down the steps, straight to a waiting auto.

It was a huge Rolls-Royce, a Silver Ghost, the most

beautiful machine ever made. The canvas top was pulled up, and the running lights were burning. A man in a uniform got out from the front and opened the rear door. He helped her up onto the big running board, and up again, holding her elbow as she scooted inside. Then he took his place at the wheel and pulled away from the curb with a saucy toot of his horn, in the fabulous rumble of six big cylinders.

"She *is* loaded," said Mother.

"And then some," I said.

Mother closed the door. She leaned back against it, the two twenties in her hand. "That was amazing, Scooter," she said. "You know, when I saw that question she wrote, I figured Mildred was someone she liked."

"Yeah, me too," I said.

She leaned against the doorframe, looking out at the street. "I was all ready to tell Mrs. Mars that Franklin and Mildred were happy together, but something stopped me."

"You were lucky," I said.

"Oh, lucky, schmucky!" Mother came in and closed the door. "I just knew it wasn't true. I felt it, or saw it, or something."

"You probably saw the look on her face."

"No, no. It was the spirits, Scooter. They actually talked to me tonight."

"Yeah, sure, Mom," I said.

"Oh, don't believe me. But *I* know the truth."

She went down the hall, and I followed her. She led me

into the séance room. "So you're not quitting after all?" I asked.

"Scooter, I don't know."

In my mind I saw the five thousand dollars sprout wings and fly away. I saw a flock of bills so big that it blocked out the sun.

"The spirits have a plan for me," said Mother. "They made that clear just now." She took off her scarf and draped it over the back of her chair. "I only wish I knew what it was."

I didn't know what to say. I watched Mother straighten the chairs and fuss with the tablecloth.

"It was the spirits who sent Mrs. Mars," she said. "They sent Grover Cleveland too." Smiling now, she held up the two twenties and kissed the little portraits of Cleveland. "What a handsome little man."

"Are you still going to see Dr. Wiseman?" I asked.

"Of course," she said.

"What will you tell him?"

"Why don't you come along and see?" she said.

10

SATURDAY, JUNE 5, 1926

EXTRA!

MADAM KING SEES THE FUTURE

It would have been easier to walk to Dr. Wiseman's hotel, but Mother insisted on taking the Steamer. "I want to go in style," she said. "This is the Ritz, after all." So she put on her goggles and hat, and we puffed up to the front doors of that swanky hotel in a whirl of white steam. A man in a uniform helped Mother down from the driver's seat. Another held the door as we passed into the lobby.

I had only seen inside the Ritz through the windows. I had never guessed I would walk through the lobby one day, under the big dome of carved wood, with the chandeliers glittering. The floor was made of slabs of pink stone, and across it—with clattering steps—ran an army of bellboys. There were tall trees, and white statues, and a staircase that was wider than Main Street.

"What a swell joint," I said.

"Shhh. Don't talk like that," said Mother.

There was a whole row of elevators with their doors pulled open. In each one, a boy about my age sat on a stool at the control lever. In their fancy uniforms and round hats, the boys looked like a row of monkeys waiting for their organ grinders.

The people that strolled through the lobby, up and down the stairs, must have been the richest in the world. There were men with spats and walking sticks, ladies in shimmering gowns. A nanny in a nurse's suit led two little girls in pigtails. A woman in red walked a little white dog no bigger than a rat.

At the front desk, the manager was wearing a tuxedo. He bowed to Mother, his cummerbund so tight that it squeaked. "May I help you, madam?" he asked.

"I have come to see Dr. Wiseman," said Mother. In fancy places, her voice turned fancy. "Would you be so kind as to tell me which room he is in?"

"Certainly." The manager put on a pair of eyeglasses and turned the pages of a big book. He bent his head and pretended to read but really gave Mother the once-over, peering slyly over the tops of his cheaters. "Room four-ten," he said.

"Thanks awfully," said Mother.

"But I believe that Dr. Wiseman is having lunch just now."

"In your diner?" asked Mother.

The manager looked pained. "Madam, he is in our restaurant."

Whatever it was called, it was nothing to sneeze at. The white tablecloths were bright as snow, the sugar bowls and ashtrays like carvings of ice. On every table was a vase of white flowers, and a single bee was buzzing through the room, flitting from vase to vase.

Waiters in white jackets were clearing away the remains of meals. At one table, two priests were tucking into a tray of tarts and cakes. At another, five pash dames in tight dresses and wide hats sprawled in their chairs like thin lizards. Their spines arched, their arms stretching, they crossed their legs and smoked their cigarettes.

Dr. Wiseman was sitting nearly in the middle of the room. As soon as he spotted us, he stood up and raised his hand as a signal. I almost laughed, because he looked like a gnome popping up from a snowy garden.

There was another man at the table, his back toward us. He used a white napkin to wipe his mouth, then folded it carefully, put it down, and stood up. He turned to greet us, straightening his cuff. It was Viktor Valerian.

His beard was so perfectly pointed that a blacksmith might have trimmed it with chisels and files, rather than a mere barber with scissors. When he bowed to Mother, he clicked his heels together. "Madam King," he said, grabbing hold of Mother's hand. He leaned forward and kissed the backs of her fingers. "Today I dine on elegance; I need no other food."

It made me want to pull a Daniel Boone. But I could see that Mother thought Viktor was a wow, despite what she thought of him as a mystic. She blushed and looked down at the floor.

Beside her, Dr. Wiseman was smoldering. It gave me the heebie-jeebies to see men being jealous of my mother.

On the table was a big plate of emptied oyster shells, wineglasses with big fingerprints on them, and a scattering of bread crumbs. The men had finished their meal, but the doctor grabbed a chair and made a place at his side for Mother. I had to fend for myself.

Dr. Wiseman put his arm on the back of her chair. His hand was just touching Mother's shoulder. "Madam, I didn't expect to see you so soon," he said. "I hope it's a favorable sign."

"I fear it is not," said Viktor. "Unless I am mistaken, Madam King is rejecting our offer."

He was pretty sharp to wise up so fast. Mother nodded.

"Was the money insufficient?" he asked.

"No. It was very generous."

"The cause unworthy?"

"Strike two," she said, with a small smile.

Dr. Wiseman looked impatient. "Do you intend to carry on as a medium?"

"I do," said Mother.

"In that case, my dear, the result will be the same." He bent his fingers so that they wrapped round Mother's shoulder. He tried to pull her closer, but only tipped sideways himself. "Now or later, you will come to the attention of

Harry Houdini. Do you have any idea what he does to a fraud?"

There was a hint of Mother's naughty smile. "Now, why should that matter to me?"

"Go and watch his show," said Dr. Wiseman. "That's all I'll say." He took his arm from the chair and leaned back with his thumbs hooked behind his suspenders.

The bumblebee buzzed behind him and flew a wide circle round the table. Dr. Wiseman watched warily until it settled on a bunch of flowers three tables away. The dames were laughing in the background, and my mother was making eyes at the Russian.

"What about *you*, Viktor?" she asked. "Are you scared of Houdini?"

"Not at all," said Viktor Valerian. "But the doctor is right. I warn you that Houdini is poison. He is not above using trickery to get what he wants. There was an unfortunate incident during yesterday's morning session, where we had a wonderful manifestation, didn't we, Doctor?"

"Oh, we did indeed," said Dr. Wiseman.

"And much levitation," said Viktor. "A vase of flowers rose from the table. Dr. Wiseman himself was floated to the ceiling."

"I felt my head touch the plaster!" cried the doctor, with a little laugh. He put his hand lightly on his hair.

"Really?" I said. We had "floated" dozens of people to the ceiling; it was easy to do. A shout from Mother in the dark—"Mr. Stevenson, you're floating!"—a pull on the back of the old duck's chair, and that was all it took. His feet would tilt from the floor, and in his mind he'd be soaring. "You're above the table now. You're going to touch the ceiling," Mother would shout, and I would give him a little pat on the head. Yes, floating someone to the ceiling was so simple that it was laughable. The Russian suddenly didn't seem so miraculous.

By the look he gave me, he knew it, too. His eyebrows drew together; his eyes got small and dark. I wasn't convinced that the Russian could float people to the ceiling, but I had no doubt that he could read my mind.

I wanted to look away, but I couldn't. It seemed we were locked together, eye to eye. Then the doctor suddenly waved his hand in the air, and that kind of broke the spell.

"They should keep bees out of here," said Dr. Wiseman. He was swiveling in his chair as the bee circled. When it came closer, he flailed with his arms.

The bee zoomed past him. It went weaving away between the tables, and Dr. Wiseman—not the least embarrassed—adjusted his tie. "Now, where were we?" he asked. "Well, I don't remember. But the point of the story is this: when the lights came on, there was black thread on the floor."

"In the séance room?" I asked.

"That's correct. Houdini pounced on it, of course. Proof of fraud, he claimed."

"As if thread could lift a man," said Viktor, laughing.

"There was a great deal of thread. Several yards, in fact," said Dr. Wiseman. "So Houdini must have planted it; there's no other explanation." He shook his head. "I've never trusted that blackguard. If I was the chairman, he never would have been named to the committee, no matter how he begged. His treachery knows no bounds."

"That man will do anything to discredit me," said Viktor. "He cannot be allowed to return to our sessions."

"Never," swore Dr. Wiseman. "Our only consolation is that Houdini's days are numbered."

I caught Mother's eye. This was the second time we'd been told the same thing. "Why do you say that?" I asked.

"Oh, it isn't *my* idea," said the doctor. "This is coming through the spirits. It's being whispered through speaking trumpets. It's being written in slates, spelled out on Ouija boards. I've heard it in Boston and London, in the South and in the West. The message has come to every medium of any worth. Houdini is going to die."

"Has anyone told him?" I asked.

Dr. Wiseman nodded. "He has been informed. No doubt he is on his guard."

I remembered Houdini ranting about his Torture Tank being put on display. It seemed he'd been right to be angry.

"That actor," said Dr. Wiseman. "That Herman Day. I believe he was controlled by the spirits. He was sent to kill Houdini."

"I don't think that's true," I said.

'What do you mean, young man?" said Dr. Wiseman, turning red. Clearly, he didn't like to be contradicted by a boy. "I suppose you know better?"

"Well, yes, sir," I said. "I think I do. I've been investigating, and I think—"

"*Investigating?*" Dr. Wiseman laughed as though I was a two-year-old who'd come out with something clever. "Young man, you're no Hercule Poirot. I've been investigating spirits longer than you've been alive, my boy. I think I know better than you." He leaned back, all smug and full of himself, and brought out his fancy pipe.

Soon great puffs of white smoke were wafting over the table. Viktor Valerian, half hidden behind them, seemed to be smiling.

"Scooter," he said, "I'd like to hear more about your little investigation. If you don't believe that spirits were involved, then what *do* you believe?"

"I'm not really sure yet," I said.

Dr. Wiseman suddenly laughed, coughing smoke. "That's some investigation!"

"Now, just a minute, Doctor," said the Russian. "Let's hear the boy out." His black beard seemed to float through the clouds of pipe smoke as he stared at me. "I read in the paper that Herman Day fell into the Torture Tank while he was trying to murder Houdini. Is that not so?"

"It's possible," I said. "But maybe someone else was trying to kill Houdini, and Herman Day just came along. Or maybe *no one* was trying to kill Houdini. Someone might have murdered Mr. Day and then tried to fix it so it looked like he was after Houdini."

"Interesting," said Viktor Valerian. "Why, that's a plot that Houdini himself might have dreamed up. It sounds like one of his dreadful motion pictures, doesn't it, Doctor?"

"It does," said Dr. Wiseman.

"So, who is your chief suspect, Scooter?" asked Viktor. "Who gained from the death of Herman Day?"

"A few people did," I said.

He raised his eyebrows. "Really? Like who?"

I figured he was putting on a show to impress my mother. But it pleased me that he was interested, even if only pretending. "Well, there was Mr. Topper," I said. "And Kitty Moore and Bobbie Baker. And Mr. Knight *thought* he would gain, but I'm not sure that he did. You know, there's other people too. There's—"

"Now, I *am* impressed," said Viktor. "I think you're on the right track there. Madam King, that's quite a boy you're raising."

"He is, isn't he?" said Mother. "Quite a boy."

Everyone sat looking at me, so I felt kind of embarrassed. I didn't explain my other ideas, and a moment later—in a puff of smoke from Dr. Wiseman—our meeting came to an end.

11

SATURDAY, JUNE 5, 1926

EXTRA! EXTRA!

Tops Topper Delighted

Mother was nervous as we came out of the Ritz. She rubbed
her arms as though the air had grown suddenly cold. She
sent a valet to bring the auto round, then stood quietly at
the curb, staring at the traffic going by.

When the valet returned, he was walking. "I'm sorry,
ma'am," he said. "But I don't know how to start a Steamer."

"Then you're a fool," she snapped.

"Mother!" I said, surprised. She had never spoken like
that to anyone.

She seemed shocked at herself. "Oh, I'm sorry," she said,
but it was too late. The valet gave her a look that told exactly what he thought of the sort of people who had lunch at
the Ritz. Then he turned quickly away, the gold fringes flapping on his epaulets.

We hoofed round the corner to the Steamer. When
Mother saw the puddle of water it had left on the ground,

she nearly burst into tears. "Oh, you stupid old thing!" she said.

"Why's it stupid?" I asked.

"Not it. Me!" she said. "Oh, Scooter, what have I done? Five thousand dollars, and I threw it away like that."

"We could go back," I said. "You could tell Dr. Wiseman that you changed your mind."

"Never."

The Russian's castle loomed above us. The sun was just gleaming out from the edge of its eaves, so we stood in the shadow of the big house. I set to work with the Steamer, fetching a jug of water from the backseat.

"Well, I made my bed; I have to lie in it now," said Mother.

I filled the boiler, put back the jug, got out the kerosene torch. I lit it with a match. The flame made a growling sound.

"Maybe I'm asking too much of the spirits," said Mother. "They've pointed me in the right direction, and now I have to figure out where to go. I think Mrs. Mars gave me that money for a reason. It's all tied up together."

I hunched down and lit the pilot light. I waved the torch along the vaporizing tube. The water that had leaked from the pipe started sizzling and boiling.

"I need to make a splash," said Mother. "I have to put my name in the papers."

As the tube heated up, the colors of the flame stretched in ripples across the metal, changing from red to blue to yellow.

"You know the problem?" she said. "He's up there, and I'm down here." She gestured with her head toward the old castle. "The rich ones like Mrs. Mars, they go to Viktor. I have to send out yellow cards to snag the ones like that. Otherwise, all I get are the Figgs and the Stevensons. I need more Mrs. Marses, that's what I need."

The water was gurgling in the tubes, the boiler starting to creak and pop.

"But they're not coming to me, so I have to go where they live," said Mother. "That's what I have to do; I just don't know how to do it."

I turned off the torch and stood up. The water was heated, the Steamer ready to go. Mother snapped her goggles into place, and we climbed aboard.

"If you get a brainwave, let me know," she said.

Mother tapped the gauges in front of her. She pumped with the water pump, then opened the steam throttle, and off we went. At the corner, she turned right, heading north past the Orpheum.

On the big marquee across the front, Houdini's name was still at the top. Underneath, it said: *Tops Topper Presents Kitty Moore*, and under *that* was a new name: *Bobbie Baker*. The hatcheck girl who called herself an actress had made the big time. It was all because someone had murdered Herman Day.

I remembered Bobbie chewing her gum, not caring at all about the body twisted in the Torture Tank. The song she had quoted came back to my mind. *Hello, Central. Give me no-man's-land.*

It gave me an idea—not a brainwave, exactly, but the start of a thought.

A trolley went by in the other direction, its bell ringing. When it passed, I had to look over my shoulder to see the Orpheum. We were already in the next block. Mother swerved through the traffic, tooting her horn at a man on a wobbly bicycle. When she stopped at a traffic light, I tapped her arm.

"Mom, you want to be famous, right?" I asked. "You want your name in the paper?"

"I guess so," she said, watching the light.

"I know how to do it."

She looked right at me, a hopeful look coming to her face. "How?"

"You have to hold a séance."

The look fell away. "Oh, that's clever," she said sarcastically. "I would never have thought of holding a séance."

"Not just *any* séance," I said.

The light buzzed, then changed colors. Mother worked the throttle, and we went bouncing across the streetcar tracks.

I pointed back down the street. "You have to do it at the Orpheum, Mom. There's a room off the lobby that you can rent for thirty dollars a day."

"Thirty dollars a *day?*" said Mother. "For that kind of money, I could rent a whole house for a month."

"Not a *haunted* house."

Mother sighed as she veered round a man with a vegetable cart. "Scooter, you're babbling."

"No, listen, Mom," I said. "It's the room where Herman Day was killed. You can rent it for a night, hold a séance there, and ask his spirit to appear."

"Why?"

"So he can name his killer."

Mother laughed. It was just a short little laugh, with her head thrown back, so the breeze caught the red curls at her forehead. "Hah! Who's the killer?"

"I'm not sure," I said. "It doesn't matter."

Her long scarf fluttered as she turned her head to look at me. Her eyes blinked behind the round goggles. "Do you really think that I can call up the spirits?"

"It doesn't matter," I said.

"Stop saying that!"

"But it doesn't," I told her. "You'll be famous for trying. The Man in the Moon will write all about it, 'cause we'll invite him to the séance. We'll invite everybody."

I thought we would argue about it for hours. But Mother suddenly grinned and said, "You know, it's not a bad idea. It's not a bad idea at all."

She looked over her shoulder, then wrenched the wheel, and we went flying to the left, over lanes of traffic. Horns blared; tires screeched. The driver of a jitney shook his fist, and bicycles collided. But Mother was mindless of it all. High on the seat of the Steamer, she went sailing down Jefferson and back toward the Orpheum.

She parked right out front, jolting two wheels onto the sidewalk. Still in her driving clothes, she marched toward the revolving door. I had to run to catch her. "Mom, wait!" I cried.

She stopped. She pulled down her goggles, letting them dangle round her neck.

"Mr. Topper won't want to rent you the room," I said. "Not when he hears what it's for."

"You don't think so?" She took off her scarf. "Let me handle this, Scooter."

We went together through the revolving door. But as soon as we were inside, she sent me away. "Go wait by the fountain," she said. "Count the dimes, or something."

The doorman came. He told Mother to stay in the lobby while he fetched Mr. Topper. She opened the front of her coat, shoved her hands in her pockets, and looked up at the giant posters. She didn't go anywhere near the easel at the end of the lobby, where Houdini's challenge listed the mediums.

I looked at the pennies and the silvery dimes shimmering under water. When Mr. Topper came into the lobby, he didn't see me. He must have thought Mother was alone.

They hadn't met before. I saw Mr. Topper pause in the doorway as he got an eyeful of the beautiful lady in a raccoon coat. He stood straighter than ever, trying to squish that big round stomach. Then he stuck out his hand and marched toward Mother. "Hello, hello. I'm Tops Topper," he said. "I'm the manager here. How may I help you?"

Mother smiled. "My name is Madam King. I—"

"Dee-*lighted*!" said Mr. Topper, beaming back at her.

134

"I'm interested in renting that room," she said, pointing. "For a séance."

"A séance? What an interesting idea," said Mr. Topper.

He kept nodding as Mother explained what she wanted, and why. Then he cleared his throat. "Well, I'll tell you," he said, "I'd like to accommodate you."

"Swell," said Mother. "I—"

"Ah," he cautioned, holding up a finger. "That room rents for thirty dollars. That's per *day*, Madam King. Thirty dollars a day." An oily smile came to his face. "Now, I'm sorry if that's too much, but—"

"Not at all." Mother opened her purse and took out the two twenties that had come from Mrs. Mars. "You can make change, I assume?" she said.

I could see that Mr. Topper had boxed himself in a corner. With a scowl and a mutter, he hauled a fat wad of bills from his pocket, pulled off the gold clip, and peeled away a ten-dollar bill.

Mother put it in her purse. "Okay, Scooter, let's go," she said.

I came out from behind the fountain. Mr. Topper looked surprised then, all right. His jaw dropped so far that I could see the fillings in his back teeth.

"You again?" he said. "Why is it that every time I turn around these days, you're right there?"

"Oh," said Mother innocently. "You've met my son?"

"Scooter *King*. Of course," said Mr. Topper. "I should have guessed."

"Well, I'll catch you later, Mr. T," said Mother. She took my elbow and steered me away.

We went round the revolving door and out to the street before she let me go. Then she looked back over her shoulder. "I don't like that man," she said. "You know, Scooter, he might be a Regular."

That took me by surprise. I could imagine Mr. Topper being mixed up somehow in the murder of Herman Day, but I hadn't thought he might have sent the card. Then I had to wonder why he would have done that, or why *anybody* would have done that.

Whoever the Regulars were, it didn't make sense that they would warn me about themselves.

12

SUNDAY, JUNE 6, 1926

PARIS PROF TURNS WATER INTO GAS
PERSIAN SHAH CROWNS HIMSELF
MADAM KING PREPARES FOR SÉANCE

We planned the séance for Wednesday at midnight. There was a lot to be done, and I ended up doing most of it.

I wrote the invitations. I got them printed and sent them out. I turned cheesecloth into ectoplasm and brewed fresh spirit lights from the heads of wooden matches. I made a list of things we needed, and right at the top was a long table and thirty chairs. So Mother sent me to the Orpheum to take care of that as well.

"Now, you watch out for Mr. Topper," she said. "Watch that he doesn't pull a fast one."

I was ready. But that day, Mr. Topper was unusually friendly. He hurried to meet me at the door and whisked me into that room of marble floors and chandeliers. He had already found a table, and it was perfect. Nearly twenty feet long, solid and heavy, it would seat everyone we wanted, with room to spare. He had a chair to match it—a huge throne with a velvet cushion, its arms carved to look like lions' paws.

"This stuff's been kicking around for years," he said. "It was last used in—" He stopped himself suddenly and lowered his voice. "The Scottish play, if you know what I mean."

"No, I don't," I said. I had no idea then that it was bad luck to say the name Macbeth in a theater. Tops just wouldn't do it.

"Let's put it this way," he said. "The ghost of Banquo sat in that chair. So it's fitting, I think, to use it again in your little séance. Should be another fine performance."

"You're not a believer?" I said.

"In your mumbo-jumbo spirit world? Not at all," said Mr. Topper. "But I wouldn't miss your séance for anything. I can hardly wait to see who shows up—both living and dead."

He went away to find some chairs, leaving me alone in the room. I looked at the lights and the way the table was turned. Mother had to be facing the door, because I didn't want anyone coming in behind her. So I dragged the big throne down the length of the table, with its legs squealing on the floor. I was just putting it into place when the stage-hands started bringing in the chairs. They were wooden chairs that folded shut, and they didn't look very fancy. But when I complained to Mr. Topper, he kind of blew his lid.

"Scooter, look," he said, with his teeth clamped shut. "This is a theater, not a furniture store. You'll have to make do."

He stalked from the room. I set up the chairs, making

such a racket that someone came in to see what was happening. She was a dyed blonde with stuck-on lashes, in a slinky gown that swept the floor. I had to look twice to see that it was Bobbie Baker, changed from a flapper to a lady. She carried a cigarette holder more than a foot long, waving it round like a magic wand. The only thing left from the old Bobbie Baker was her chewing gum. She smacked away to beat the band.

"Gee, what did you say to Tops?" she asked, looking round the room. "You got him all bent out of shape."

"Really?" I asked. "All I said was that I didn't like the chairs very much."

"Yeah, that'll do it." She blew a small bubble, then opened her mouth and sucked it in. "Doesn't take much to get an old actor worked up."

"Mr. Topper was an actor?" I said.

"Sure. A good one, too." Bobbie walked down the table, the cigarette holder waving in her hand. "He gave it up to make money instead. Not many actors make money, you know."

She fell into the big throne at the head of the table. She waved the cigarette holder above her head. "Thanks for the invite, by the way. Who else is coming?"

"Everyone," I said. "We invited all our regular sitters, and Mrs. Mars, and the newspapers, and—"

"Houdini?"

"Sure," I said. "We figured he'd come anyway, even if he wasn't invited."

Bobbie laughed. "That's probably true." She wriggled in the chair; she crossed her legs. "So your mother's the medium, huh? Is this where she's going to sit?"

"Yes," I said, putting the last chair in place.

"Do you think Herman will really come back?" asked Bobbie. "Will we see his spirit standing here?"

"I hope so," I said.

She stroked her fingers along the wooden claws of the carved chair. "Say, can a spirit touch people?"

"Sure."

"Can it hurt them? Could a spirit kill a person?"

She asked all this still chewing her gum. The bubbles—like her questions—kept popping out. They appeared and disappeared from between her red lips, so she looked like a fish puffing air. Then suddenly she got up and—with another flourish of her cigarette holder—headed for the door. As she passed me, I saw that her cigarette was really made of wood. Its glowing tip was only painted to look like ashes.

"Hey, Bobbie?" I said.

She turned back at the door.

"Do you know where Melvin Knight is staying?" I asked.

"Sure. He's down at the Union." Bobbie laughed, bursting a bubble. "And out. He's down and out at the Union."

The Union was the oldest hotel in the city. It was six stories high, made of stone that had turned brown, like old teeth. Pigeons loved to perch in all the cracks and niches in

140

the walls, and old men gathered on the bench outside its door, cackling at people who passed.

"Why is Melvin Knight staying in a place like that?" I asked.

"Why do you think?" said Bobbie. "You wake up one morning with no job and no money, you don't check into the Ritz."

"But he was famous," I said.

"That was yesterday," said Bobbie.

I went straight from the Orpheum to the Union Hotel, past the bench of old men, into a dingy lobby. There was a dead palm tree in a big red pot that people had used as an ashtray. From the smell, I figured the old men had used it for a toilet too.

In every way, it was the opposite of the Ritz. Instead of a huge and fancy desk, there was a little counter behind a cage of metal bars. And instead of a man in a tuxedo, there was a lady in a housedress, with wire curlers in her hair. She stared out at me through the bars, coughed twice, and asked, "What do you want?"

"I'm looking for Melvin Knight," I said.

"Six-ten."

Instead of an elevator, there were stairs. Old newspapers lay strewn on the steps, torn and trampled by feet. I went up in a zigzag, back and forth from floor to floor. I tried not to touch the banister.

There was no door on the landing at the sixth floor. Or,

rather, there *was* a door, but it was lying on the carpet, its hinges torn from the wall. I walked right over top of it and down a corridor that stank of cats. At room six-ten, I heard a radio playing. I knocked on the door.

"Come in!" shouted Melvin Knight.

He was sprawled across the bed in a rumpled suit, lying on his back, looking up at a strip of flypaper that hung in a coil from the ceiling.

"I'm Scooter King," I said. "I met you at—"

"Yeah, I remember," he said.

"I wanted to give you this."

From my pocket I took out his invitation to the séance. It was still sealed in the envelope, with his name on the front, but no address. I took it to the bed and held it out for him, but he didn't lift his hand to take it.

"Is it a bill?" he asked.

"It's an invitation," I told him. "To a séance. My mother's a medium, and—"

"My mother's a large."

Well, that was an old joke. I didn't laugh, and neither did Melvin. He kept staring at the flypaper while the radio played a ragtime tune.

"She's having a séance in the Orpheum," I said. "She's going to contact Herman Day."

"Why bother?"

"To ask who killed him."

"Whatever he says, don't believe it. The man was such a liar," said Melvin.

He patted the pockets on his jacket, then pulled out a packet of matches and half a cigar. The matches were from the Limelight Club. The cigar was broken in the middle but held together by a Band-Aid.

One-handed, he opened the matchbook and struck a match. "You know something, kid?" He lit the cigar, then blew a big ball of smoke up toward the ceiling. "When those flies get trapped, they'll pull off their own legs to get free. Isn't that something?"

I looked at the coil of yellow paper. There was a fly stuck near the top, flailing away to the ragtime music.

"I like to see 'em squirm," said Melvin. "Reminds me of the theater."

He blew another puff of smoke. "The funeral was today. Did you know that? I was the only one there who knew him. It was just me and a priest and a rotting corpse. The rotting corpse was a lawyer. He read the will. You know who got the money?"

"You?" I asked.

Melvin glanced at me. "That's right. How'd you know?"

"Just a guess," I said. "It was nice of him to do that."

"It was a dirty trick," said Melvin Knight.

The music stopped. There was a jingle for laundry soap, then Gene Austin started singing "Everything Is Hotsy-Totsy Now."

Melvin groaned. "I put a lot of work into hating that guy, and in the end he pulled a fast one. Now I got to feel bad for the rest of my life. Lucky he left me a packet, so I don't have to work while I'm feeling bad. I can feel bad while I'm lying on the beach in Florida."

"Then why are you staying in this crummy room?" I said.

"I don't get the money for a couple of months." Out of his mouth came a cloud of smoke. "I don't know why; something to do with lawyers."

"Do you want to come to the séance?" I asked.

"Yeah, sure. Maybe I can ask the rat a question. 'Hey, rat, what were you thinking? Why did you want to kill Harry Houdini anyway?'" Melvin tapped his cigar ashes onto the bed. "Nothing makes any sense, kid. Why would he want to do something like that?"

Maybe Melvin was drunk. Maybe he missed his partner a whole lot. I couldn't say one way or the other, but he sure looked miserable. Above his head, the fly stopped struggling, and Melvin sang along with the radio: "No more crying, no more sighing. I'm through with the blues."

I left him with his misery in his two-bit room with the radio playing. I went home and had dinner.

It was probably right then, as I ate my shepherd's pie, that the Man in the Moon was typing out the column that the whole city would read in the morning. His fingers must have been pounding the keys, the little levers flying up at the paper, the ribbon chattering along, the carriage hitting its stop with a ping of the bell. He had heard of my mother, and his first item told all about the séance.

On Monday morning, my mother screamed when she

saw her name in the paper. She woke me with that shriek, and I thought the house was on fire. It smelled of smoke and burnt bread. I ran downstairs to see what had happened.

Mother was standing at the kitchen counter with the newspaper in one hand, the butter knife in the other. Gray smoke was boiling from the doors of the toaster, but she didn't even know it. She just stood there reading the paper, with a wedge of butter sliding down the knife blade.

"Mom, the toaster!" I said.

She looked into the smoke. "Oh, my goodness!" she cried. But she didn't put down the paper. She pulled the electrical plug from the wall, then tipped the whole toaster into the sink. The doors fell open; the toast slid out like black shingles, and Mother just reached across and pushed the window open. Smoke billowed around us.

"Listen to this!" cried Mother, as though nothing had happened. She held up the paper and read aloud. 'Madam King will be chasing spooks at the Orpheum on Wednesday. Seats at her table said to be the hottest thing in town. Don't tell Izzy Einstein, but spirits will certainly appear.'"

"Who's Izzy Einstein?" I asked.

"Oh, Scooty!" She gave me one of her funny looks. "He's that cop in New York who raids all the speakeasies."

I got a tea towel and chased away the smoke. I poured out the Pep, had my breakfast, met the mailman at the door. In all that time, Mother didn't move from the counter. She leaned against it, reading that same item over and over.

"This is it, Scooter," she said. "This is the big time now. Oh, I wish my mother was here to see it. Her own daughter written up in 'The Man in the Moon.' Imagine that."

I saw Mother grinning, and thought it was probably the happiest day of her life. But something nagged inside me that it wasn't going to last. I had a kind of superstition that too much happiness wasn't lucky.

Mother was itching now to get down to the Orpheum. She wanted to study the room, to sit in the big chair with its carved paws. "I have to feel the atmosphere," she said. "I have to know if Herman's spirit lingers there. Go get the Steamer started, will you?"

I kept quiet about my bad feeling. Mother would only have scoffed at me anyway, because *she* thought that everything was hotsy-totsy now. When she found a parking place right outside the Orpheum, she thought it was more than good luck. "Oh, the spirits are looking after me," she said.

We went through the revolving doors, past the fountain and the big posters. Mother saw the long table and chairs in the other room and made a beeline for the door. She passed the easel beside the door, stopped abruptly, and took two steps back.

She was gawking at the white placard as I came up beside her. I saw right away what had caught her eye. At the bottom of the card, squished into the last inch of space, was the name "Madam King."

When she spoke, her voice was small and frail. "He's coming after me," she said.

I didn't know what to tell her. I scrunched down inside myself, because I figured it was my fault she'd been added to the list.

Mother groaned. "Scooter, we've put him on my trail." Her happiest day had just become her worst. She had turned pale, and her hands were shaking. "Dr. Wiseman was right," she said. "I should have taken the money and the challenge. I should have listened."

"I'm sorry," I said.

"Well, it's too late now." Mother looked grim. "We're going to have to make this the best séance that anybody's ever seen."

13

MONDAY, JUNE 7, 1926

SHIPWRECK KELLY TRIES FOR
  FLAGPOLE RECORD
GANGSTER GUNNED DOWN IN NEW YORK
HOUDINI TAKES ON LOCAL MEDIUM

That afternoon, Mother took the rest of her forty dollars and went on a spending jag. She bought herself a cloche hat that made her look two inches taller and a boa that she could whirl three times around her neck.

"It makes a girl feel good to dress up," she said. But it didn't really make her all that happy.

We went to see Houdini's show. Ten minutes before the curtain went up, we took our seats in the auditorium. They were crummy seats, so close to the wall that we looked nearly sideways across the stage. Mother sat peering around like a pigeon, then started picking out the mediums and the fortune-tellers in the audience. "Why, there's Mrs. Snale," she said, pointing to a little prune of a person in the front row. "Of course, Viktor's not here."

That night, Bobbie Baker was the first act. As a hat-check girl, she was pretty good. But as an actress, she wasn't.

She came hoofing onto the stage in tap shoes and did a strange little song and dance for the opening number while people took their seats. With her arms flapping like noodles, her lips bent up in a fake smile, she looked like a Raggedy Ann being tossed around the stage.

Next was Kitty Moore. She sang the same songs I'd heard her sing before. She might not have had the best voice in the world, but up there on the stage, with every spotlight aimed right at her, she looked like a million bucks. There was not a sound in the audience until she finished; then the men stood up, whistling and clapping, and she did her little curtsies at the edge of the stage, blowing kisses all over the joint.

Tops Topper came out from the wings, clapping his hands as he walked. He made a big announcement that he was booking Miss Moore for a month. After that, he said, she would be going on the circuit as a headliner, off to Chicago and New York and Seattle. "I'll be going with her," he said. "I'm her manager now. Remember that this is where she got her start, right here on this stage!" He swept his arm toward her. "Ladies and gentleman, a star has been made!"

He backed into the shadows, clapping again, leaving the stage to the brand-new star. And—wowzers!—did she sparkle! She glowed and gleamed and glittered as the spotlights whirled around her. The orchestra started up with its trumpets and drums, and down from the balcony fell a red rain of tossed roses.

In the morning paper, the Man in the Moon would call

her a thief because she'd stolen the show. Right then, we didn't want her to leave. So she did an encore, and then another, and no one minded that Harry Houdini was kept waiting for nearly half an hour. Except Houdini himself.

I could see him pacing back and forth at the side of the stage, out of sight of nearly everyone else. When he finally came out, he looked angry. He ripped the sleeves from his coat with a particular fury and hurled them down into the orchestra pit.

He did his magic in the same fierce way. I was amazed all over again by the threaded needles and the bullet in his teeth. I held my breath along with everyone else when he was lowered into the Burmese Torture Tank. I grew nearly frantic with waiting. I was on my feet, shouting with a hundred others, when Houdini—soaking wet—stepped out from behind the screen and tossed an armload of chains and shackles onto the stage. There was such a clamor of applause that it hurt my ears. Then Mother leaned over and said, "I was hoping he'd really drowned this time."

We stayed in our places during the intermission. Then Houdini—dried and changed—came to the front of the stage. "Ladies and gentlemen," he said, "I will show you things tonight that no one has ever seen. I will take you where no one has gone except in darkness. Follow me . . . to the séance room."

Behind him, the curtain picked itself up from the bottom and soared above the stage. A table and two plain chairs were set up in the middle, looking very small and lonely. A hand bell, a tambourine, and a speaking trumpet stood on the black tablecloth.

Houdini asked for the house lights to be brought up. He shaded his eyes and stared out into the audience. Leaning forward, he looked up and down the rows.

I jumped up and waved my arms. "Mr. Houdini!" I shouted.

Mother tried to pull me down. "What do you think you're doing?" she said.

But I wasn't the only person doing it. Here and there, others were clamoring too. Houdini looked out at us and pointed right at me. "You. The boy," he said. "Would you help me, please?"

People clapped for me to go. Mother was holding my coat, so I just shrugged it off and shuffled out to the aisle. An usher appeared, to lead me to the stage.

We went up by the stairs that Houdini had shown me. But now dozens of people worked in a frenzy in the wings and the workshops. There was a man on a stool at a little desk, who seemed to run the show. He snapped his fingers, and a girl came running. She straightened my clothes; she combed my hair. Another girl dabbed my face with powder that made me sneeze. Then I was pushed out onto the stage, and people laughed as I stumbled into view. It was hot as heck up there, in the glare of lights. Half blinded, I could see only darkness where the audience sat. Houdini shook my hand. He asked my name.

"Scooter King," I said.

He didn't let on that we'd already met. He put me into one of the chairs at the table, and he sat in the other himself. Then he and I reached across the table and joined hands, as though we were sitting for a séance. "Put your feet on mine," he said. "Keep pressure on my toes so that you know I don't leave my chair."

I straightened my legs until our feet overlapped. I pressed hard on his toes.

"Oh, I almost forgot," said Houdini. "You have to be blindfolded."

One of his many assistants came out with a black cloth. It was the lady who had come dancing from the giant radio cabinet. She stood behind me and tied the cloth over my eyes. I could see only sparkles from the bright spotlights and a dim shape that was Harry Houdini.

"Now we begin our séance," he said. "I call on the spirits to show themselves."

Nearly right away, the tambourine jangled. Its little cymbals clashed right beside my ear, and I jumped in my chair. The audience started laughing, and they didn't stop for twenty minutes. I kept holding Houdini's hands, touching his feet, so I was sure he didn't move from his chair. But I heard whispers in the speaking trumpet and the clammy touch of spirit hands on my face. Houdini even told me that I was floating toward the ceiling, and—though I figured he was lying—I couldn't help ducking my head. The audience howled.

I thought Houdini had assistants all around me—one to

bang the tambourine, another to work the trumpet, a third to touch and tickle me—because everything happened so fast. But when he told me to take off the blindfold, we were still alone on the stage. I was still holding his hands and feet, and strewn around me were reaching rods, balloons, and cheesecloth faces. I felt hot from the lights, dizzy from the noise, but I loved being up there in front of the crowd. I thought it was the bee's knees.

The orchestra started playing, and the curtain dropped in front of me. I could hear the crowd moving, everyone talking all at once.

Houdini stood up from his chair. He leaned over the table and put his hand on my shoulder. All around us, stage-hands were bustling. "Do you know why people were laughing?" he asked.

"Not really," I said. "What did you do?"

"A bit of flimflammery; a bit of fraud," said Houdini. "Just the usual sort of séance business, you know."

I felt a little sting from that, as though he'd slapped me. "How many people were helping you?" I asked.

"No one."

"But I controlled your hands," I said.

"You *thought* you did."

"And your feet."

"False shoes." Houdini lifted his foot onto the chair to show me. He was wearing a shoe that looked ordinary, but it broke open at the heel, letting his foot slide out.

"My toes are as nimble as my fingers." He couldn't stop himself from boasting. "I worked a reaching rod with my foot, and everything else with my hands. People laugh when they see how easily it's done. In daylight, it looks rather silly, don't you think?"

He got me out of the chair and led me from the stage. Two men went running past to take away the table.

"Are you trying to embarrass me?" asked Houdini.

"No, sir," I said.

"Well, what then? Why are you holding a séance in the theater?"

"I want people to hear about my mother," I said.

"Oh, they will. I promise you that," he said. "Now, look. I haven't time to talk just now, but I want you to come and see me. Will you do that?"

"What about?" I asked.

"Just come and find out."

We had reached the top of the stairs, but even there we weren't alone. The stage manager was racing around with a clipboard. Mr. Topper was trotting behind him, while stagehands and assistants were swarming like bees. In the auditorium, the house lights dimmed and brightened. The orchestra was warming up again.

"Listen," said Houdini. "Don't tell your mother we've had this talk. When you come, come alone. Do you understand?"

"Yes, sir," I said.

"Now get back to your seat."

I ran down the stairs. In the auditorium, people called out to me. They nudged each other and pointed my way. "There he is," they said. "There's that boy." I felt like a star.

As I squeezed down the row of seats to my place, people clapped me on the back. Men shook my hand; women ruffled my hair. "Good show!" people said. But Mother was angry. She glared at me, tight-lipped.

"What's wrong?" I asked. I was busting to tell someone all about Houdini, and it was disappointing to see my mother like this.

"He made us all look like fools," she said. "And you helped him. Thank you very much."

The orchestra stopped playing. A thick sort of silence settled over the place. At the back of the hall, somebody coughed.

Along the stage, the curtains rippled. Then Houdini swept them apart and stepped out to the front of the stage. He combed his hair with his fingers and stood smiling down at everyone.

"Oh!" said Mother. "He thinks he's so *clever*."

Houdini looked serious now, like a father about to give his children a lecture. He spoke in a loud voice. "There is in this city a Madam MacGregor, a medium who earns ten dollars a sitting with the same trickery I have shown you tonight. She claims to have a gift. Yet she is nothing but a fraud."

A woman stood up in the audience and shrieked back at him, "You're a liar!"

"Who says that?" barked Houdini. He shaded his eyes from the spotlights and leaned forward, staring into the audience. "Who calls Houdini a liar?"

"I do." The woman was wearing a white boa and a hat with tall feathers. "I call you a scoundrel as well. And a dog! And I warn you to be careful!"

My mother squeezed my arm. "That's her. It's Jean MacGregor."

"To be careful of *what*, madam?" asked Houdini.

"Of what you say!" cried Mrs. MacGregor, her feathers quivering. "I have friends who will come up to the stage. You will get a beating."

"Your friends will *not* come up to the stage. I will *not* get a beating," said Houdini. He stepped back, spreading his arms to include all of the audience. "Friends, let me tell you about Jean MacGregor. Let me tell you how she reunited my assistant with his dead sister and his dead mother—my assistant who *has* no sister, whose mother still lives."

Everyone laughed at that.

"Don't listen to him," said Jean MacGregor, staring round at all of us. "He's lying through his teeth."

"She diagnosed my friend with a very strange illness," said Houdini. "I can tell you he's never been ill a day in his life, but she—"

"Liar!" cried the medium.

"But she put him at death's door. She gave him a month to live. Oh, but there was still hope! There always is with these charlatans! Why, no sooner did she diagnose him than she offered to cure my very healthy friend. She could restore his vigor, she promised, with nothing more than a candle and a magnet, for nothing less than twenty dollars. She would have put him on a reducing diet, making him a good deal lighter in the pockets."

I couldn't help feeling sorry for Mrs. MacGregor. In the end she fled in tears, running with her white boa streaming, the feathers shaking on her hat. She reminded me of a little quail racing for cover.

I looked at my mother, saw the look of shock on her face, and suddenly felt horribly, terribly cold. It was awful to think of her being singled out and torn apart in the same way.

As Mrs. MacGregor vanished through the doors, Houdini called out another name. Another medium stood up. It was Madeline Wick. But instead of waiting to be drawn and quartered, she held her pocketbook up to her face and fled on the heels of Mrs. MacGregor.

"Oh, this is horrible," said Mother. "Scooter, I've seen enough. I want to go home."

14

TUESDAY, JUNE 8, 1926

HULA HOOPER IN HOSPITAL
MONKEY TEACHER GOING BACK TO COURT
HOUDINI, SCOOTER STRIKE A DEAL

First thing in the morning, I went to see Houdini. I met Mr. Topper in the lobby of the Orpheum, and he sent me down to the dressing rooms. "You know the way," he said. "Just go ahead. It's the first room on the right."

It was exciting to go down there by myself, past the workshops and everything. I almost hoped that someone would shout at me, "Hey, kid! Where do you think you're going?" just so that I could stop, turn slowly back, and say in a voice like ice, "Houdini is expecting me."

But no one shouted; no one stopped me. Before I knew it I was down in the long corridor, with the rooms on either side. The first door on my right had a brass star screwed to the wood. Underneath it, someone had stuck a bit of tape and written "Houdini." I knocked as lightly as a spirit.

"Come!" said Houdini from inside.

The room was larger than I would have guessed. There

was a table and chairs, a long closet full of clothes. There was a white sofa where Houdini was sprawled, with his feet on the cushions, below a wall full of photographs. Bess was putting on makeup in front of a mirror surrounded by lights. With a tiny brush in her hand, she was painting black around her eyes. She saw me in the mirror and smiled.

"Ah, Scooter," said Houdini. He was still in his dressing gown, with brown slippers on his feet. There was a newspaper in his hands and a small stack of them on the floor. "Thank you for coming. I had hoped I might see you last night."

"We left early," I told him.

He chuckled. "The mediums often do. Frankly, I'm not sure why they show up at all." He dropped his newspaper and sat up straight. "Bess, it's Scooter and his mother who are tossing the séance here."

"Yes, Harry, I know that," she said, dabbing with her brush. "Why don't you tell the kid to sit down?"

"Of course. I'm sorry." Houdini waved me into a chair at the table—one of Mr. Topper's little folding things. I had to be careful not to nudge the table, as it was piled to overflowing with papers and books, with a big typewriter balanced at the edge. "I'm told your mother will try to reveal the killer," he said.

"Yes, that's right," I told him.

He nodded. "Have you ever heard of Garnett, Kansas?"

"No, sir," I said.

"We played there in ninety-seven, Mrs. Houdini and I. We were just starting out, and not yet very successful."

"Boy, you can say that again," said Bess.

Houdini ignored her. "We played at the old opera house. The town was abuzz because a woman had been murdered in the town, so I announced that Mrs. Houdini would name the killer. I got her seated on the stage, and I covered her with a sheet." Houdini made a flourish with his arms, as though casting down the sheet. "Bess announced that she was going into a trance. I asked her about the murder. She could describe where it happened because we'd read about it in the paper. I asked, 'Can you see the killer?' 'Yes,' she said. I shouted at her," and he shouted again, "'Tell me his name!'"

At her mirror, Bess answered. It was as though the two of them were back on that stage, reliving a moment nearly thirty years old. Still holding the brush, Bess closed her eyes and talked in a dreamy sort of voice. "His name is . . . His name is . . ."

"Yes, tell me!" roared Houdini. "Who is it? Tell me now!"

"It's . . ." Bess let her head tip sideways, then collapsed onto the counter, scattering her little bottles of makeup. Then she sprang up again, laughing.

"That's how it ended," said Houdini. "She never named the killer, but that didn't matter in the least. We were a sensation! So we began to tour as mediums. I called myself Professor. Sometimes it was Mrs. Houdini who had the powers, sometimes myself. We pulled the same trick in Galena in ninety-eight, and—"

"Harry, he's not interested," said Bess.

"All right," said Houdini. "The point is that you don't

fool me, Scooter. I know your tricks. You might say that what you do in the séance room is harmless, that you sell pleasure and hope. But I see it differently." He shook his finger at me. "You take money by trickery. What it comes down to is that you're no different than a pickpocket, and I can't let that go unchallenged."

I couldn't believe that Houdini had called me in only for a lecture. Inside I was burning, but I stood and listened.

"When I was young, my father died," said Houdini. "I believed that I could speak to him again if I went to a medium. I didn't doubt it. But I couldn't afford a medium. So I sold the only thing I had of value—the watch my father had given me—and I went to one séance after another. At every one I was duped. My pockets were picked again and again."

"You'd think he'd learn," said Bess. She had moved on to the lipstick now, and was pouting at herself in the mirror. "But it was the same thing all over when his mother died."

"Not quite," said Houdini. "Of course I went back to the mediums. I was in utter agony. But I was wise to their tricks by then. I *expected* to be cheated. And they tried. Anyone else might have been fooled, but not me; not Harry Houdini."

"But he keeps looking," said Bess.

"I do," said Houdini. "I keep searching for that miracle: a real medium who can let me speak once more to my mother."

"What about Viktor Valerian?" I asked.

Houdini's expression darkened. "He's a fraud," he said.

"But I'm having trouble proving it. You know about our incident with the length of thread."

I pretended that I didn't, but that only made Houdini angry. "Now, look here," he said. "I know you had lunch with the Russian and the doctor."

"How do you know that?" I asked.

"There are many things I know that I don't let on that I know." His blue eyes seemed as fierce as a hawk's. "I searched Viktor myself, and I know for a fact that he was not carrying that thread. So someone must have planted it, and I suspect that someone was Dr. Wiseman."

"Unless Viktor's on the level," I said.

"A slim chance," said Houdini. "That doctor's a meddling fool. He's a wily old bird. He'll stop at nothing to get me removed from the committee. Well, Dr. Wiseman deserves to be put in his place, and I'm the one to do it. I'll fix his wagon, you'll see."

"Harry, please don't talk like that," said Bess. "Don't get so worked up."

She seemed a very kind person, very gentle. Houdini smiled at her, and the redness left his face. He began walking slowly round the room, looking at the photographs on the wall. He reached out to straighten one. "The committee is giving me the high hat now," he said. "They're meeting without me, holding trials without me. I'm afraid they'll give the prize to a fraud."

"What will you do about it?" I asked.

"Well, more to the point," said Houdini, "is what *you*

will do about it." He turned to look at me. "I was hoping you would take on a little job."

"Wowzers!" I said. "What kind of a job, Mr. Houdini?"

"Have you ever heard of the Secret Service?" he asked.

"Sure," I said.

"Well, I have my own secret service," said Houdini. "Let me tell you, it's bigger and better than the real one."

"Oh, Harry!" said Bess.

"It's true," said Houdini. "I have thousands of agents. All over the world. Come and look at this, my boy."

I went to his side, and we stood together in front of the pictures. They were all photos of himself, shaking hands with different people. I recognized Charlie Chaplin, and Mary Pickford, and a whole bunch of others. There was even a picture of Houdini shaking paws with Rin-Tin-Tin.

"These people are all in my secret service," said Houdini. "They are my eyes and ears, always on guard against spiritual frauds. Scooter, would you like to join them?"

"Wow. You bet!" I got so excited that Bess laughed. But Houdini only smiled.

"Good." He put a hand on my shoulder. "I want you to go to Viktor's séance on Thursday afternoon. Don't make yourself obvious. Just watch and listen. Pay attention to everything and everyone in the room. Then let me know what you see. All right?"

"Yes, sir."

"If you do well, I may overlook your mother. I might 'forget' to expose her."

He made it sound like a generous offer, and I tried to act pleased.

"Now punch me in the stomach," said Houdini.

I couldn't believe I'd heard him right. "Pardon me?"

Bess spoke up at the same time. "Harry, don't do that."

"It's all right." He spaced his feet apart, drew back his elbows, and faced me squarely. "Go ahead, Scooter. Give me your best shot. Try to floor me."

"I'm leaving," said Bess. She dropped her lipstick on the counter, stood up, and left the room.

Houdini didn't move. His eyes grew narrow, his smile very strange. "What are you waiting for?" he said. "Hit me, Scooter."

I felt a bit silly doing it, but I made a fist and socked him one, right in the breadbasket. He didn't even grunt. It was like punching a sandbag.

"Harder," he said. "Put some muscle in it. Don't be a willy boy."

I hit him as hard as I could. I gave it to him straight in the gut, and I thought it would knock his lights out. But he was as solid and thick as a half-frozen snowman. The only thing that got hurt was my hand.

"I can do a hundred and fifty push-ups," said Houdini. "Jack Dempsey could hit me and I wouldn't feel a thing."

Just a few days ago, I had thought that it would be almost impossible to meet Houdini. Now I found out that the hardest thing was getting *away*. He made me look at every photograph. Then he got out his scrapbooks and showed me every page, and each book was nearly as thick as a Bible. He launched into story after story. I finally made my escape when we came to the end of the third scrapbook, when he got up to get the next one.

I practically ran from the room. I headed down the corridor, making straight for the rear exit. The bits of tape fluttered from the doors of the dressing rooms. I read them as I passed, and stopped when I saw the name of Herman Day.

I figured that if Herman's name was still on the door, then maybe his things were still inside. There was no telling what I could learn about the guy if I could see what books he'd been reading, what keepsakes he'd kept beside his bed. I looked up and down the hall, then reached out and turned the handle.

The door clicked open. I found a room half the size of Houdini's, a pretty sad sight. Herman might have dashed out just a few minutes ago, 'cause everything was in its place. A bow tie and a belt were hung over the back of a chair. A pair of slippers was waiting by the door like a couple of patient little dogs. But the toes were scuffed away. In the corner was a wardrobe trunk, cracked open, showing a few wooden hangers and even fewer clothes.

The counter was far smaller than Houdini's, the mirror scratched and chipped. There was an artificial head that must have worn Herman's toupee at night, a jar of face cream, a glass of water half finished. There was an ashtray with a picture of Niagara Falls on the bottom. Herman had used it to store a few coins from his pockets and a button that must have popped off his shirt. A pair of spectacles was placed beside it, their thick lenses magnifying the patterns on the countertop.

On the table by the bed was a magazine. Herman Day had been reading *Life*.

In a quick look around, I saw all that I wanted to see. I didn't go into the room; I didn't poke or pull at things. I closed the door, then went on down the hall and out through the back of the Orpheum.

I half expected to find Tops Topper waiting for me again, or to see Viktor Valerian staring down from his high castle. But I came out on the usual razzle-dazzle of people and motorcars, with nobody lurking and nobody watching.

I started home with a new problem to keep me thinking. The way I figured it now, Houdini was wrong about Herman Day. That poor little man had never tried to kill anybody.

15

WEDNESDAY, JUNE 9, 1926

WORKERS ON STRIKE IN WARSAW
MUSSOLINI WOWS EUROPE
ORPHEUM SÉANCE PROVES POPULAR

On Wednesday night, everything was ready. The Orpheum was the perfect place for a séance.

The first person arrived at five minutes to eleven, and the rest came trickling after. The marble floor and the high ceiling gave an unsettling echo to every voice and footstep. Whispers seemed to come from corners, movements from the shadows. As midnight approached, people kept looking uneasily over their shoulders, like so many deer watching for wolves.

My mother was waiting in Mr. Topper's office, ready to make her grand appearance. Everyone we'd invited had shown up, and I was certain that somewhere in the room was the killer of Herman Day.

Sergeant Summer was there, scoffing down the little sandwiches I'd laid out on a table in the lobby. Houdini had come in his morning coat, but with a strange vest underneath. It reminded me of the clothes I always got for Christmas from my dotty aunt Melba, and I wondered if Bess had made it herself. It had a bulge in the middle, and an odd-size button that stood out like a sore thumb. Houdini kept standing like Napoleon, with one hand tucked in his jacket, as though he was trying to hide that vest.

Melvin Knight smoked his cigar in a lonely corner, looking more uneasy than anyone else. Bobbie Baker stood talking with Bess Houdini, while Tops Topper and Kitty Moore might have been tied together at the elbow.

Mrs. Figg and Mrs. Hardy and the Stevensons were there. They kept in a little group and didn't talk to anyone else. The Stevensons, especially, seemed to go out of their way to avoid me. Whenever I got close, they turned away like a school of fish.

Mrs. Mars arrived with her chauffeur. He brought her into the room, then glided out so quietly and quickly that it seemed he had vanished in midair.

Viktor Valerian and Dr. Wiseman arrived together, and *that* got the feathers flying. Houdini challenged them at the door. "Are you always in collusion?" he asked.

The Russian was tall enough that he could glare down at Harry Houdini. "Are you always suspicious?" he replied. Then he held out his arms, as though to be crucified. "I suppose you want to search us now. No telling what you'd find."

"I'd find a fraud. And a fool," said Houdini.

Dr. Wiseman pulled them apart. He gave me a chilly look as he led Viktor across the room.

The last to arrive was a man I'd never met. He wore a pirate's black patch over his left eye, while his left arm was missing altogether, the empty sleeve pinned up to his shoulder. But he was friendly and happy, and he held out his one hand to shake mine firmly. "Evelyn Bird," he said. "Known as the Man in the Moon. Nice crowd you've got tonight. Say, is that Tops Topper with diamond studs on his collar and a dame on his elbow? Have to see him. Catch you later." Off he went, greeting everyone in the same way.

At five minutes to midnight, I lit the candles. There were a dozen of them spaced along the table, and I'd spent more than an hour getting them ready. Each one had been cut in two, and rejoined with a bit of the wick taken out. I figured they would all burn out together, except for the one closest to my mother. That would be the first to go.

At four minutes to midnight, I got everyone in their places. I made sure that Dr. Wiseman was on my mother's left-hand side, because he would be easy to fool, and that I was on her right. I wanted Mrs. Mars beside me, on account of she was partly blind. Then I put Houdini at the end of the table, as far from Mother as I could get him.

At three minutes to midnight, I turned out the lights. I went to the lobby and brought in my mother. Everything was planned to the minute, so she was ready and waiting.

She was wearing black, of course. Her face seemed to float in the darkness as she settled in the chair. The candle flames twisted toward her, then straightened again.

"Join hands, please," she said.

She talked about the power of the circle and the terrible things that would happen if it was broken. She led us in the Lord's Prayer, than announced that she was going into a trance.

In that big wooden chair, she moaned and hummed. We could see her face drifting in and out of the candlelight as she moved forward and back. Her eyes were closed, her lips barely moving.

Mother timed it perfectly. At midnight precisely came the chiming from the church clock on Madison. At the first stroke of the bells, Mother fell silent. At the last, as the dying sound tingled in the room, her eyes suddenly flew open.

"I have made contact," she said. "The spirits are among us."

She leaned back into the darkness, then forward again to the flickering light. When she spoke, it was in the girlish voice of Dorothy. "I have come to lead you through the spirit world. Is there someone you would like to speak to?"

My mother answered in her trance voice. "There is. We seek the spirit of Herman Day, who died in this very room."

"A young man?"

"Not old."

"Is he newly arrived in Summerland?"

"Within days," said Mother, her voice changing back and forth, old to young.

"Yes. I believe he is coming."

A tingly feeling came over me. It was part of every séance, and I believed that it was shared by every sitter at every table. I thought of it as the feeling of waiting for something to happen. But people such as Mrs. Figg would say it was the arrival of the spirits.

The candle sputtered at the head of the table. The flame shrank, then went out. I figured there were ten seconds until the others followed.

"Are you with us now?" asked Mother, in her trance voice. She answered in Dorothy's: "The spirit is afraid of the light."

"Put out the candles, then," said Mother. "Make the spirit welcome."

In a moment, of course, and nearly together, the candles snuffed out down the length of the table.

I felt Mrs. Mars tighten her grip, squeezing my fingers. "I feel it," she said. "There's a presence."

"Yes," said somebody else.

I could see nothing—only blackness. But out of that dark came a hand, and it touched me. Fingers suddenly squeezed my shoulder.

I nearly jumped out of my skin. But it was only Dr. Wiseman, muttering into my ear.

"Scooter," he said, "will you change places with me, please?"

"Why?" I asked.

"My hearing." He tapped the right side of his head. "It isn't very good in this ear."

Stupid old man, I said to myself. It annoyed me that he was polite when it suited him. But I remembered how he'd

173

leaned sideways to talk to my mother, how he'd cupped his hand to his left ear, and I believed him. So I got up and changed places, moving behind my mother's chair to the spot between her and Bobbie Baker.

The actress smelled of perfume and hair spray. "Who's that?" she whispered as I took her cold little hand. "It's like musical chairs in here."

The movement and voices were upsetting for Mother. They put her off her stride, so she had to start over. "The circle has been broken," she said. "I will try again to summon the spirits."

She had to use her left hand now to pull the little bottle from its pocket in her dress. I heard the click of glass against her teeth as she pulled out the stopper. A sudden green glow seemed to pour from her mouth.

Round the table, people gasped. "Spirit lights," said someone. Another voice began a faint mumble: "The Lord is my shepherd . . ."

No matter how many times I saw them, spirit lights always amazed me. I brewed them myself, from nothing but water and the heads of wooden matches, making a liquor that didn't look like anything more than colored water as long as it was sealed in a bottle. But as soon as air was let in, the liquid seemed to come alive, pulsing with that light.

Mother made it float up in the darkness, as high as she could reach. Then she brought it slowly down, replaced the stopper, and lifted it again. Even to me, right beside her, the green glow seemed to hover there, unsupported by anything natural.

With the bottle closed, the light went out again. It faded gradually, so that it seemed the spirit was actually moving away from us, withdrawing to its shadow world. When it went black, Mother dropped the bottle in her lap.

"Herman Day," she said, in her spooky voice. "We ask to speak with the spirit of Herman Day."

I heard a creak from the wooden chairs, then the squeal of its legs on the marble floor. I tried to peer through the darkness but couldn't see a thing. The sounds seemed to come from the far end of the table, and I feared that Houdini was freeing himself from the circle.

Mother must have heard the same thing, but she didn't break the trance. "Herman Day," she said, "if you are with us, please give us a sign."

I could feel her left foot moving. It nudged my chair, and then my ankle, as she felt for the heavy wooden leg of the table. "Herman Day, are you with us?" she asked.

In Dorothy's young voice, she answered her own question. "There is a spirit in the room."

"Who is it?"

"A man," said Dorothy. "He's scared and lost. He hasn't found his way to Summerland yet. He wanders between two worlds."

My mother asked, "Is it Herman Day?"

"It is," said Dorothy.

"May we speak with him?"

"He's waiting now. He's standing by somebody's shoulder."

"Have him send a sign that he's here."

A loud tap trembled through the table. Somebody shouted, "He's here!" There was another tap, and another— six or seven all at once.

"Stop!" cried a woman. "Send him back!" said another.

But my mother didn't send him back, and she didn't stop. She had never given a better séance. Even I had to remind myself that the tapping came not from another world but from the metal plate in the side of her shoe.

A clammy unease settled around the table, a looming sense of danger. Bobbie Baker was squeezing my hand so hard that my fingers were being crushed together.

"Come amongst us, Herman Day," said my mother. "You are not bound by the world of the living, or trapped in the world of the dead. You are free to wander wherever you like. Reveal yourself, Herman Day!"

Somewhere in the room—or beyond the room—a different tapping began. It was either very faint or very far away, and it came with a steady swelling, like the drums of a distant parade. Then it broke into a shifting, raggedy pattern.

I broke out into a cold sweat as I realized what I was hearing. In the blackness, on the marble floor, someone was tap-dancing.

This wasn't in our plan. Mother had meant to channel a

spirit, not materialize it. Our hands were touching, so I knew she was still beside me. I stared into the dark for a flicker of movement. When the sound of dancing faded away and Mother went on with the séance, her voice was shaky. I imagined her wondering what had happened.

"Listen to me, Herman Day," she said. "Is the person who killed you here in this room? Is the killer with us now?"

One tap came through the table.

"Can you name that person?" said Mother.

She was supposed to tap again. But, instead, a voice came whispering from the darkness. It was a man's voice—definitely not my mother's.

"Hello, Central. Give me no-man's-land."

It was the most frightening thing I'd ever heard, a creaky voice that raised goose bumps on every inch of my skin.

"That's him!" said Melvin Knight. A woman screamed. Dr. Wiseman shouted out, "No! No, please!"

There was a burst of light. It was blinding and burning, a huge explosion of white light. In an instant, the room was full of smoke—of smoke and shouting and noise. Chairs tipped over, women shrieked, and Sergeant Summer was yelling above it all, "That's it; we're quits. It's all over, see. Someone turn on the lights right now!"

My eyes were full of smoke and white spots. I moved toward the door, feeling through the darkness. But Mr. Topper knew just where to find the switch, and the chandeliers came on as I was still groping my way along the wall.

I blinked and rubbed my eyes. I could smudge out the spots but not the smoke.

A woman screamed behind me. "Madam King has collapsed!" she said.

Sergeant Summer shouted, "No one move. It's murder!"

16

WEDNESDAY, JUNE 9, 1926

EXTRA!

MYSTERIOUS FIGURE FOLLOWS SCOOTER

The smoke cleared away rather quickly, floating up among the chandeliers. But it took a moment for my eyes to get used to the light.

The first thing I saw was my mother slumped facedown on the table, and a crowd of people behind her huge chair. Mrs. Stevenson was right at her side, trying to lift Mother's head. She was the one who'd asked for help, and she kept on asking now.

But everyone ignored her. My mother had only fainted, but Dr. Wiseman was dead.

He was sprawled back in his chair. His arms dangling at his sides, his neck oddly bent, he stared unseeing at the chandeliers. A look of horror was frozen on his face.

"I was holding his hand!" cried Mrs. Mars. She was nearly hysterical. "I could feel the life go out of him. I think the spirit snatched away his soul."

"Think again, sister," said Sergeant Summer. "Spirits don't break people's necks, see. They don't leave marks like this!" He pulled Dr. Wiseman's collar from its studs, and we saw the bruises—finger-shaped—burned into the man's skin.

"Someone came up behind him, see. Reached down and throttled him," said the sergeant. "Someone with the eyes of a cat."

"Maybe," I said. "Maybe not." A sudden thought made me shaky in the legs. I held on to the big wooden chair as I came up to Mother's side. Mrs. Stevenson moved away to give me room.

"Mom?" I said, leaning down. "Mom, are you all right?"

Her head was turned sideways, her cheek squashed on the table. When I saw her mouth all twisted, I thought for a terrible instant that she'd had a stroke. But I shook her by the shoulder, and that jarred her out of whatever state she was in. Suddenly, she bolted upright in her chair, drawing a gasp of breath. She looked at poor Dr. Wiseman. "Is he dead?" she asked.

"Deader than dodos," said Sergeant Summer. "Now, look here. Someone in this room is a killer, see, and no one leaves this building until we find out who it is. It might take all night—I don't care—but I want to interview every one of you, see."

Harry Houdini was standing by himself at the far end of the table. He spoke loudly but calmly. "That won't be necessary."

In his hand was a bit of metal and wire with a wooden

grip. I knew it at once as a magnesium flash holder, for the taking of photographs. The light and smoke had come from a coil of metal that had burned—in an instant—to a little gray worm of ashes.

Houdini set his contraption on the table. We all watched as he took off his morning coat and folded it carefully onto the back of a chair. Underneath was his strange vest with its stranger button in the middle. But neither was what it had seemed to be. The vest had no back, and the button wasn't a button at all.

With a magician's gesture, Houdini ripped off that bit of clothing. It was more like an apron made to *look* like a vest, fastening with straps round his shoulders. Hidden behind it was a round case made of metal.

"A detective camera!" said Sergeant Summer.

"A Spearman." Houdini held it up for all to see. It was like a small cake tin, and the button was its lens, mounted right in the middle of the circle. "This little gadget has been the ruin of half a hundred mediums, and I suspect it's about to ruin one more."

"How dare you!" cried my mother.

"Madam, if you're innocent, you have no worries." Houdini unfastened the camera from its straps. "I'll take this round to J. J. Doyle's right now, and we'll see soon enough what happened here. I suspect the plate is not the only thing that will be exposed."

"Just a minute, Mr. Magic," said Sergeant Summer. "What did I just tell you? I don't care if you *are* the great

Houdini. You could be the great Moses on the mountain for all I care. No one leaves this joint till I say so, see."

Houdini was nearly steaming. He talked with his teeth clenched together. "If you don't trust *me*, send somebody else."

"I will go," said Viktor Valerian.

"You?" Houdini laughed. "You're the last person I'd trust."

Sergeant Summer seemed fed up. "Will you two quit your bellyaching?" he said. "Give the kid the camera, see. The kid can take it round to Doyle's."

"No!" shouted Tops Topper. He had been watching from the other side of the table. "I don't believe that's a good idea."

"Why not?" asked Houdini.

"To send a boy by himself? Why, it isn't safe." He *did* look frightened. The tip of his tongue came out, darting across his lips. "Tell you what—I'll go with him. Or I'll go alone. Okay?"

"Look, you bunch of bozos," said Sergeant Summer. "Ain't Doyle's only a few blocks away? Now give the kid the camera, see, and get him outta here!"

Houdini took me to the door. He put the camera into my hands. "I'm entrusting you with this," he said. "Go straight to Doyle's and get him out of bed. He knows the camera; you won't have to explain. Tell him that Houdini needs the prints right away. Understand? Right away."

"Sure." I didn't need to be told every little thing.

"Take Union Street. That's the fastest way."

It bothered me to be sent off with a push, as though I was a little kid. So I went particularly slowly, hoping that Houdini was watching me. But all it did was give Mother a chance to come after me with a warning: "Scooter, you don't have to go if you're scared."

"I'm not scared," I said.

"Well, be careful. Remember the Regulars."

I moved more quickly then. I was nearly at the door when I heard Sergeant Summer bellowing. "Tops, you got a telephone in your office? I want to call for the meat wagon, see."

Mr. Topper said, "Help yourself," but the sergeant kept shouting. "Send everyone in one at a time. The rest can wait here, see. Or out in the lobby—wherever they want."

I went out to the street and headed north toward Doyle's.

Anyone could have followed me. Anyone at all. But I didn't even think about it until I turned onto Union Street, three blocks away.

It was the oldest street in the city, narrow and dark, paved with red bricks. Walking on those bricks made a sound like a clock, steady and loud. I found it comforting at first, because the place was kind of spooky. But just as I got to the darkest part, another clock started ticking behind me. Someone was dogging my steps.

I stopped. So did the sounds. I looked back but saw only shadows.

"Who's there?" I called.

Nobody answered.

The buildings on either side were made of brick and gray stone. Here and there were the ghosts of old advertisements painted on the walls. Every window on the ground floor was sealed up, and the ones above them were black and empty. Union was a deserted canyon.

At either end of the block, pools of yellow light shone a few yards into the street, and motorcars went back and forth. But where I was, the only light came from the stars, in a silvery slit high above me. I had never felt more alone in the city.

"Hello?" I called again.

I watched for a long time for someone to appear, but nobody did. Then I started on my way again, and the person followed, step for step.

Every few yards, a set of stairs went into the ground, leading to doors below the street. They made dark little caves that had spooked me when I was a kid and now nearly scared me to death. I imagined someone lurking in every one.

Again I stopped, and again the person stopped behind me.

"Who's there?" I said again.

I heard the coo and flutter of pigeons, a flock disturbed by something. A shadow moved, and something like a big dog darted from a stairwell. I turned around and ran.

The person came running after me, taking two or three steps now for each of my own. But I didn't look back. I ran and ran, with Houdini's camera spinning on its strap, banging against my leg. I passed the dark doorways and the boarded windows, with the clocking of footsteps coming faster and faster.

Ahead was the glow of lights from Seventeenth, the motorcars and the sounds of people. I thought I couldn't make it that far before hands reached out from behind and hauled me down. There was a stitch in my side, an ache in one leg, and I couldn't breathe hard enough—or fast enough—to go on for very long.

Then I stumbled on the bricks. The camera, swinging back, slammed against my knee. The jolt of pain nearly knocked me down. The camera flew away ahead of me, skittering over the ground. I snatched it up and staggered out to Seventeenth, into a circle of light.

I nearly collided with a man on a bicycle. I sent him reeling into the street, where a motorcar screeched to a stop, blaring its horn. Without a glance back, I turned to my right and bolted for Doyle's.

I didn't stop until I reached his doorway. Then I leaned against the wall until I could breathe properly, until my heart had slowed. I raised my fist and pounded on the door.

Mr. Doyle came down in slippers and pajamas, with an old coat on top. He put on his little spectacles and blinked at me. His voice had a thick Irish accent. "And who might you be?" he asked. "And why are you knocking me up in the middle of the night?"

I lifted the camera.

He squinted at it. "Why, that's Harry Houdini's," he said.

"What do you think you're doing with Harry Houdini's camera?"

"My name's Scooter King. Mr. Houdini told me to bring this to you," he said. "There's a picture inside, from the séance tonight, and he needs it right away."

A woman called down the stairs, "Who are you talking to, Jimmy?"

"Just a lad named Scooter!" he shouted up at her. "Go back to sleep, woman."

"Tell the lad he's got no manners," she said. A door slammed shut above us.

"Well, she'll be sleeping like a baby now," said Doyle. "Plugs in her ears, and a wee dram in her throat." He took the camera, then glared at me sharply. "Why, look at that! You've cracked the lens!"

He tried to show me, but I couldn't see what he meant. "Someone was chasing me," I said. "I dropped it."

"You've probably cracked the plate as well. You'll be lucky if there's a picture at all," he said. "Well, I'll see what I can do. No point in you waiting here, though; I wouldn't trust you to carry it back."

I didn't feel like arguing. Besides, he didn't give me a chance. He went away with the camera, leaving me to shut the door myself. I went back to the Orpheum—but not along Union—and found it almost deserted. Only three people were sitting in the lobby: my mother, Tops Topper, and Sergeant Summer.

My mother—the "psychic"—didn't even guess that anything had happened. "I'm glad you're back," she said. "Now we can go home."

"Where's everyone else, Mr. Topper?" I asked.

"Most of them, they went down to the—" He clammed up, looking sideways at the policeman. I figured they'd gone to the Limelight Club but he didn't want to say so with a badge right beside him.

Sergeant Summer pulled out his black book. He had taken the names and addresses of everyone at the séance, and added mine and Mother's at the bottom. "Now scram," he said. "You too, lady."

We had a lot of time to talk as we started the Steamer. Mother sat in the driver's seat, her scarf wrapped round her shoulders. She was pretty shaken up, on account of Dr. Wiseman being murdered at her séance.

"It was my fault, wasn't it, Scooter?" she said. "He would still be alive if I hadn't held that séance."

"But *you* didn't kill him, Mom." I was filling the boiler with water, dribbling a small stream into the gutter. "You can't blame yourself for that."

"Well, maybe," she said. "But he'd still be alive if I hadn't invited him."

"And *I* might be dead." I tossed the empty jug into the backseat. "Mom, I think the killer was after *me*. When the lights went out, Dr. Wiseman was in a different chair. I switched places with him in the dark."

"Oh, my goodness." Mother put her hand to her mouth. "Scooter, I never even thought of that. You're right; you were probably the target."

"I guess the killer was trying to get me out of the picture," I said. "He must think I'm getting close to figuring out who he is. You know, someone even followed me to Doyle's."

"Who?"

"I don't know. It could have been anybody, Mom." I lit the torch and crouched on the road.

"Do you think it was one of the Regulars? Or someone from the séance?" Mother leaned over the door, looking down at me. "Say, you don't think one of the Regulars was at the séance, do you?"

"Mom, I don't know," I said. "But we'll find out tomorrow who the killer is. As soon as Doyle exposes the plate, everyone will know."

But that never happened. Sometime that night, as we were driving home in the Steamer, J. J. Doyle was murdered.

17

THURSDAY, JUNE 10, 1926

PRESIDENT COOLIDGE HAS NO COMMENT
WOMAN SMASHES CROSSWORD RECORD
SCOOTER KING FLEES POLICE

Mother closed up the house like a fortress that night. She locked the doors and latched the windows, then started stacking tin cans on the stairs.

"What's that for?" I asked.

"Just to be safe," she said.

I didn't see how a pile of tin cans would keep us safe. All it really did was make me lie awake for hours, listening for the crash of tin cans. I could see a gleam of light under Mother's bedroom door and figured she was doing the same thing.

The noise never came. No one broke in. So maybe, in a crazy way, the tin cans did their job.

I got up early in the morning. Mother woke me by unstacking the cans. When I got downstairs, I found her at the front window, peering out between the curtains. "What are you doing now?" I asked, making her jump.

"I'm watching for the paperboy," she said.

She saw him coming from half a block away, unlocked the door, and dashed out to meet him. She snatched a paper right from his bag and left him gaping after her as she came dashing back again.

The big headline made her gasp.

MAN STRANGLED AT SÉANCE

She spread the paper on the table and leaned over to read it. She didn't see the other, smaller headline until I pointed it out.

"Oh, Mom, look," I said.

POLICE PROBE MURDER
J. J. DOYLE FOUND DEAD

According to the *Herald*, Mr. Doyle had been murdered in his darkroom. Someone had slit his throat with the edge of a glass negative and had left him to bleed to death on the floor. *His wife, upstairs, heard nothing*, said the paper. *She discovered the body early this morning.*

"Should have used tin cans," said Mother.

She went and locked the door again. She tightened the curtains where a slash of sunlight was coming through. Then she fell into her chair at the table.

"Scooter, I'm scared," she said. "I think they're closing in on us."

"Who?"

"I don't know," she said. "The Regulars, whoever they are. The killer."

Just seeing her frightened, frightened me. I remembered the sound of footsteps in Union Street, the sight of the figure bounding from the darkness. The way I'd felt then, I felt again now.

"Someone's watching us. We know that," said Mother. "Then Dr. Wiseman gets murdered right beside me. And someone follows you into the night and kills the man you talk to. Oh, Scooter, how's it going to end? What will happen next?"

Her last question was answered right then.

We heard the thud and creak of someone tramping up the front steps. The floor began to tremble.

Mother turned toward me. "Scooter, who's that?"

It was a man, for sure—and a big man too. As he crossed the porch, *everything* trembled: the lid of the percolator, the spoons in their drawer, the drinking glasses on the shelf. The windowpane rattled, and the reading lamp swayed on its pole.

He banged on the door.

Mother and I looked at each other. Neither of us moved.

The man banged again. "Police!" he shouted.

"It's Sergeant Summer," I said.

Mother laughed, but it was an awful sort of laugh. She sounded like a cackling hen. "What a relief!" she said, getting up. "You wouldn't believe what I was imagining."

I didn't go with her to the door. I flipped over the paper, turned a few pages, and found "The Man in the Moon." Of course, he talked about Mother. *Spook seekers at Madam King's séance got more frights than they bargained for. When lights came on, lights were out for Dr. Samuel Wiseman. But dead doc doesn't stop committee . . . Last trial for Viktor Valerian comes this week. Some say it's a cinch he'll get the prize.*

There was more, but I didn't get to read it. Mother called to me from the hall. "Scooter, come here."

Her voice sounded funny. I knew right away that something was wrong. I ran from the kitchen and down the hall, and found her standing with the door still open. Sergeant Summer was right on the threshold, halfway into the house. Mother was hanging on to the door as though she would collapse if she let go. I had never seen her so worried, so frightened.

"Mom, what's the matter?" I asked.

"He's come for *you*," she told me.

"What do you mean?"

Sergeant Summer stepped into the house. He was so tall that he had to make like a turtle, hunching his shoulders. Even then, his hat brushed the top of the doorway, tipping sideways. He reached up to straighten it.

"Scooter King, you're under arrest," he said. "For the murder of Jimmy Doyle."

My mother cried out, "No!"

Sergeant Summer reached round to the back of his belt. With a jangle of metal, he produced a pair of handcuffs.

They swung from his hand, glinting in the morning sun. "I gotta cuff you, kid," he said. "That's the rules, see. Now turn around, and don't try nothing, see."

I didn't turn around. I didn't move at all. "You can't arrest me," I said. "I never killed Mr. Doyle."

"That's not what his wife says, see." The sergeant opened the handcuffs. They made a ratcheting sound. "She heard him talking to a boy named Scooter. And the next thing she knew, he was dead."

"Well, sure, I was *there*," I said. "Everyone knows I was there. But all I did was give Mr. Doyle the camera, like Houdini told me."

"Tell it to the judge," said Sergeant Summer. "If you didn't do it, you got nothing to worry about, see. Now turn around, kid, or I'll turn you round myself."

"You keep your hands off him!" shouted my mother. "He's just a boy."

"So was Billy the Kid."

"Now, look!" She put her fists on her hips. "You can't come barging in here and—"

"Keep out of it, sister." The sergeant stepped toward me, and I moved back.

"Sergeant Summer, please," I said. "Let me speak to my mom for a minute. I might not see her again for a while."

"You're breaking my heart," he said.

"Just for a minute?" I asked. "Please? We'll sit at that table right in there. Look."

I pointed at the séance room. The sergeant put his head

in the door. He would have seen the table and chairs, and the gramophone in the corner.

"Yeah, okay," he said. "You got one minute. That's sixty seconds, see." He tapped his watch. "Sixty seconds starting now."

Mother and I went into the room. I tried to close the door behind us, but Sergeant Summer wouldn't allow it. He put a big fist in the way. "Door stays open," he said. "I'll be right here in the hall."

He moved toward the vestibule, but no more than three feet from the door. Mother and I sat at the table. We talked in low voices. "Mom, I didn't kill anybody," I said.

"Oh, Scooty, I know that." She held my hand, squeezing hard. "It will all be cleared up in no time; don't worry. I hate to think of you going to jail, but—"

"I'm *not* going to jail," I whispered. "I'm going to look for the killer."

"But how . . . ?"

"Keep talking, Mom." I got up from my chair.

She didn't understand right away. But as soon as she saw me heading for the wardrobe, a small smile came to her face, and she started blabbing.

"There, there," she said. "Don't worry, Scooter. I'm sure it will be all right."

I opened the wardrobe and stepped inside. With a push, the panel in the back swung aside. I waved to Mother, closed the wardrobe, and crept away through the kitchen. I went out the back door as quietly as I could. I climbed the

194

fence and jogged north along the alley, heading for the Orpheum.

I figured *someone* had to help me, and Houdini seemed my best hope.

I used the theater's back door, trying to avoid Mr. Topper, and went straight to Houdini's dressing room. He was out, but Bess was there. It was pretty obvious that I'd woken her up. She blinked at me in the doorway, scratching her head. "Gee, I don't know where he is," she said. "Did you look backstage?"

The place was nearly deserted at that time in the morning. From a long way away, I heard the sound of hammering in the workshops. I followed it to a big space behind the stage, where the Burmese Torture Tank sat covered by tarpaulins. There were other things there, all Houdini's: the table he used for his séance demonstration, the giant radio cabinet that always produced a dancing girl, the birdcage that made her disappear. The tapping went on and on, but there was no one there to make the noise.

It was creepy. Tools were lying on the workbench. The big birdcage was hollow, the radio cabinet was open. It seemed the sound had to come from the Torture Tank, from behind the brown tarpaulins. But I was frightened to lift the cloth or pull it aside, in case I saw Herman Day behind the glass, tapping with his dead man's fingers.

"Hello?" I said.

I felt that I was back in Union Street, calling out to shadows.

"Hello?" I said, a little more loudly.

The tapping stopped. I heard Houdini's voice asking, "Who's there?"

"It's Scooter King," I said.

The doors rattled on the radio cabinet. I whirled to look, just in time to see Houdini appear from thin air, stepping out of the empty cabinet. There was a small hammer in his hand and a couple of bronze nails pinched between his lips. He spat those out on his palm. "I wish you could see the look on your face," he said, laughing.

"How did you do that?" I asked.

"Let's say it's magic." He put his hammer on the workbench. "So what's on your mind, Scooter?"

"I'm in big trouble," I said.

"How's that?"

I didn't think, but just blurted it out. "Mr. Doyle was murdered, and the police think I did it."

Houdini fell back against the workbench. The little nails dropped from his hand, plinking onto the floor. "Doyle is dead?" he asked.

"Yes, sir," I said. "Someone cut his throat with part of a glass negative."

Houdini winced. He touched his neck, as though his own throat had been slashed.

"Mrs. Doyle was upstairs, but she slept right through it," I said.

We heard people walking, coming toward us. From a distance away, Mr. Topper called out, "Houdini!" He came a bit closer, and called out again, "Houdini, where are you? There's someone to see you."

"I bet he's bringing Sergeant Summer," I said. "Please, don't let him find me."

"I'm not about to." Houdini moved to the side of his radio cabinet. "Step right in there," he said. "And don't say a word."

I could hardly believe it would do any good to go into that empty cabinet. But I went where he showed me, and the next thing I knew, I was standing in darkness, closed all around by solid walls. I heard Tops Topper and Sergeant Summer come into the room. They asked Houdini if he'd seen me. "That kid with a spook for a mother," said Sergeant Summer.

"You mean Scooter King?" asked Houdini.

"Yeah, that's the one. If he shows up, you tell him something from me," said the sergeant. "Tell him he's finished, see. He can't hide forever. Sooner or later he's going to come crawling out, like a worm in a rainstorm. And then I'm going to squash him, see. You tell him that."

"Anything else?"

"That'll do."

"Then good day."

When the two were gone, Houdini let me out. It was an awkward moment, because I had learned the secret of his cabinet. "Not more than half a dozen people have seen what you just saw," he told me.

"Don't worry. I won't go flapping my gums about it," I promised.

"Then we're square." He smiled. "So what's next, Scooter?"

"I'm going to find the killer," I said. "I think I know who it is."

He nodded. "I see. And you came to ask for my help. Is that right?"

"Well, sort of." It was true that I'd wanted his help, but I figured I could find the killer without him now. "You see, I was in a bit of a fix," I said.

"A *fix?*" He laughed. "Listen, there isn't a day that goes by when I don't put myself in a fix. I might get someone to lock me in handcuffs and chains, then seal me into a canvas bag inside a metal box and pitch the whole works in a river. Now, if that's not a fix, I don't know what a fix is. But when everything's filling up with water and I'm sinking to the bottom of the river, do I ask anyone for help? Do I?"

"No, I guess you don't," I said. He didn't understand that I didn't need him anymore.

"Life's the same, Scooter." Houdini took a handkerchief from his pocket. He rubbed at a spot on the cabinet. "When a person gets himself into a jam, he better get himself out. If you can't do that, then maybe you're not the sort of person I want in my secret service after all."

Houdini looked me right in the eye but said no more. I figured he was finished with me, so I turned around and lammed out of there. I ran down the corridors and out the back door, and there was the wooden castle towering above me on the bluff. It seemed that everything had started on the day I'd gone up there with Mother, when I'd followed the Stranger to the top of the stairs. I wished I had never heard of Viktor Valerian. I wished I had never gone to his stupid house.

But I knew I had to go back. I had made a promise to Houdini.

18

EXTRA!

Bolshevik Hosts Mysterious Séance

The old man in the tricycle chair came to the door when I knocked. He was bundled in the same blankets, with the same dark glasses on his eyes, as if he'd parked himself in a closet all the time I'd been away.

"Name?" he said, in that voice like a frog's.

"Scooter King," I said. "I came with my mother last week."

He backed the chair and spun it around in its whir of electricity. "Come this way," he told me.

Again, I had to hurry after him, round the corners, past the narrow windows looking over the city. He led me to the same room as before, the huge space with the black walls, with Viktor's cabinet in the middle.

I had arrived early, but already there were nearly a dozen people in the room. The oldest was a woman in black, with a face like a windfallen apple. She sat alone in a straight-backed chair, turning a string of wooden beads through her fingers. It made a ticking sound as each brown bead fell against the next one.

I walked right around the cabinet, looking again for panels in the walls. I looked inside, at the chair still chained and locked to the floor. I looked underneath; I looked at every side. I even stepped right in and sat in that chair, so that I could see what the Russian would see when his séance began. I searched for loose nails, for secret compartments. At last I was satisfied.

When I got out of the cabinet, I came face to face with the Stevensons. All three of us drew back with little gasps and twitches, like the stooges of vaudeville. It made us laugh stupidly.

Something was different about them. Before the midnight séance that had brought the Stranger, the Stevensons had always been friendly to me, making a point to chat for a moment. At the Orpheum séance, they had kept their distance. And now it seemed that they didn't want to be with me. There was a creepy sort of silence while we all looked at things in different directions. Mr. Stevenson found a bit of thread to pull at on his sleeve.

"On a busman's holiday, are you?" he asked.

"What do you mean?"

"It's just an expression, Scooter. When the bus driver's on holiday, he rides the bus, you know?" Mr. Stevenson chuckled uncomfortably. "I had no idea you came to Viktor's sittings."

"Same goes for me," I said.

He chuckled more loudly. "Yes, I suppose so!" Then he looked down at his feet and started rubbing the toes of his shoes together.

"It's only our second time here," said Mrs. Stevenson. "Don't think we're cutting your mother loose. Don't think that's what we're doing."

"Not at all!" said her husband.

"We adored the séance last night," she said.

Mr. Stevenson touched my arm. "Here, I'll leave you to chat," he said, and made his escape.

I wished I could do the same thing. But Mrs. Stevenson looked pretty sad all of a sudden. "Scooter, listen," she whispered, watching her husband's back. "It was Paul Revere. That's what put my Henry off your mother."

"Huh?" I said. "What about Paul Revere?"

"You know Henry's a bug about him," she said. "When we got home from your mother's séance last week, he went straight to his library. He hauled out a big, thick book, and he showed me something."

"What?" I asked.

"Well, first, you didn't see the spirit of Paul Revere. You weren't at the table. You didn't see him gallop through the room on a big black horse. It had fire in its eyes. He was shouting, 'The British are coming! The British are coming!'" Her voice was a high little whisper. "It was spine-tingling, Scooter."

I nodded impatiently. "So what did Mr. Stevenson show you?"

"Oh, his book," she said. "I don't remember the title. But it said it's a myth that Paul Revere went around shouting that the British were coming. That's just not true."

"He must have said something."

She nodded. "'The regulars are out.' That's what he said."

Well, that floored me, and then some. I must have stood gaping.

"I know it's hard to believe," she said. "But Mr. Stevenson showed me in the book. The regulars were British soldiers. That's what they called British soldiers in those days, the regulars."

I remembered how Mr. Stevenson had seemed so quiet that night, while the others had bubbled away about the spirit and his horse.

"I tried to tell him there was a reason," said Mrs. Stevenson. "I said maybe the spirit of Paul Revere didn't remember what he said that night. After all, it was a hundred and fifty years ago! But Mr. Stevenson didn't believe me, so I said maybe the spirit was only saying what he thought we thought he ought to say. Do you know what I mean?"

"I think so," I said.

"But Mr. Stevenson didn't believe that either. He can be so pigheaded sometimes. He said he was through with Mrs. King. I had to beg him to go to the Orpheum."

"Did he send me a letter?" I asked.

"No." She frowned. "Why would he want to do that?"

I didn't know what to make of it. I was happy that the Regulars were just old soldiers, old redcoats dead for more than a century. I felt pretty stupid that the card had given such grief to Mother and me. I had been eluding gangsters for nothing. But I had to wonder: if Mr. Stevenson didn't send the card, then who did? I figured it must have been the Stranger.

At the end of the room, the old woman in black was still working her beads. She turned them in an endless circle, muttering all the time. Other people were coming into the room, and the chairs were slowly filling.

"Now listen, dear." Mrs. Stevenson squeezed my arm. "Don't let on that you saw us here, all right? It would disappoint your mother if she knew we came to Viktor's."

"I won't tell her," I said.

"That's a good boy."

She went tottering away to sit with her husband in the front row of chairs. I wandered right around the room, looking at all the knickknacks on all the little shelves. I studied the toy piano that had started to play so strangely the last time I was in the house. Every now and then I heard the whine and rumble of the tricycle chair as the shriveled old man brought somebody else to the room.

I didn't see the Stranger come in. I was looking at a toy train—a tin model on a bit of track—when I got the prickly feeling that somebody was watching me. I turned around, and there he was, on the far side of the room, nearly hidden by Viktor's black cabinet. Like a pair of cats, we stood and looked at each other for what seemed a long time.

In a room full of people, in the bright light of the lamps,

I was frightened. The Stranger seemed to be the sort of person who lurked in shadows and darkness, and to see him appear gave me the whoops and jiggles. Without a nod or smile—with no expression at all—he looked back at me.

I gave him a cheeky little wave. It was the best I could do, to make him think I wasn't scared. He jammed his hands in the pockets of his big overcoat and shuffled away to look at the photographs on the walls.

A few minutes later, the tricycle chair came rumbling back. Footsteps came with it, and Viktor Valerian swept through the door.

He seemed even more imposing than the last time. His hair and beard had the shiny blackness of wet coal, and his clothes were perfect. A red flower was tucked into his buttonhole, while his collar studs were like bars of silver. Just by standing there, he brought silence to the room, an end to the chatters and whispers.

His gaze flitted from person to person, lingering on some, but for no more than a moment. It touched us all like a ray of heat, as though his eyes had phosphorous in them. Below his black brows, above his black beard, they glistened brightly.

"Take your places," he said in his deep voice. "We begin."

The man in the tricycle chair closed the doors as we chose our seats. Some people had favorite spots, so there was a bit of squabbling here and there. Viktor paid no attention, but went straight to his cabinet. He stepped inside and sat on the chair in a jingle of chains. He closed the door.

In our rows, we waited. For twenty minutes nothing happened. Then a table lamp flickered. It went out, came on, and went out again. Then all the others followed, in a wave of darkness that began at the far end of the room and rolled toward us. A hundred bulbs went out in order, as though a great blanket had been pulled over the room.

The strange blue glow began to pulse in the cabinet. It floated up and hung in the air, throwing weird shadows round the room. Its color made ghastly corpses of the old women around me.

I looked toward the toy piano, expecting it to play. But its keys stayed still. Instead, in the corner, a phonograph wound itself up. I saw its handle turning, its big trumpet swivel round. Then out came thin and scratchy music—that old song "The Sheik of Araby."

The lady beside me gave a startled cry. "Look, a spirit!" she said.

A white face was peering out through a gap in the curtains of Viktor's black cabinet. As soon as I saw it, though, it was gone again. Then another appeared—and vanished. A hand came out—suddenly two hands at once, at opposite ends of the cabinet. Over the top of the curtain flew bunches of flowers. Out came a child's top that went spinning across the floor. We heard the laugh of a little girl—a shimmering, giggly sound. Then a toy hoop rolled itself through the curtains and went wobbling toward the door until it suddenly collapsed on its side. The girl laughed again, the sound coming from everywhere at once.

I saw the Stranger leaning forward in his seat. Ladies were fanning themselves, men mopping their brows. Nothing happened again for such a long time that it seemed the performance was over. People began to turn to each other, to talk in whispers, to laugh little laughs.

Then suddenly, a black telephone hurtled over the wall of the cabinet, spinning end over end. It crashed on the floor with a jangle from its bell, a clatter of all its pieces. It tumbled and rolled toward me and came to a stop maybe three feet away.

It was the newer sort of candlestick phone, with a dial at the bottom that could be turned with one finger. The cup-shaped receiver had of course fallen from its hook, and now rolled slowly back and forth at the end of its wire, like a fat mouse with a very long tail.

That telephone lay at my feet. Then, impossibly, it started to ring.

The sound jolted through the room. There was no connection, no wire, but the thing lay there and rang and rang. It quivered and rocked as it did it.

I felt foolish, and not a little uneasy, as I leaned forward and picked it up. I could feel the vibrations of the little clapper. But that stopped—and so did the sound—as soon as I grabbed the receiver. I brought the base closer and spoke into the mouthpiece. "Hello?" I said warily.

What a creepy voice it was that answered! It crackled and whooshed with electricity, as though it traveled millions of miles to come through the receiver. It was a bit like the voice of the crooner on the phonograph, rather high and strained, and so creepy that it made my skin crawl. I believed beyond doubt that it was the voice of a real spirit.

"There is a woman in the room," it said, "with the initials J.V. I wish to speak to her."

I looked behind me and to either side. Through the telephone came a crackle of sound, and then that voice again. "She sits three chairs to your right."

Beside me was a man, and beside *him* was a girl. Next was a woman in green, old and shriveled, like some sort of plant from a forest. I asked her, "Are your initials J.V.?"

She gasped, then held out her hand for the telephone.

I could hear the message coming through it, the little voice chattering away. I saw the expressions change on her face, from dread to joy to fear. Then the telephone rang again, and on it went to someone else. In that way, it was passed back and forth, from row to row, and the eerie voice gave out its messages.

As it passed the Stranger and went on down the row, I got up and went to the cabinet. Nobody stopped me. The voice from the telephone didn't ask what I was up to. I went right to that cabinet and pulled open the curtain.

I could hear the tinny little voice from the end of the room. But in his chair in the black cabinet, Viktor Valerian seemed to be deep in a trance. I could see his chest slowly expanding as he breathed, the cloth of his shirt puckering, his buttons moving. Other than that, there wasn't a muscle that twitched, an eyelid that flickered. Even his lips, I was sure, never moved. But his eyes were open, and they were like the dead eyes of Herman Day, staring—like a fish's—right at me. I let the curtain fall closed and went back to my chair.

The Stranger was watching me now. He looked boldly right at me, his green eyes shining in his spectacles. I didn't try to stare him down. I sat in my chair and watched the cabinet, wanting to believe in Viktor Valerian.

The messages kept coming. The telephone made its way to the old woman with the beads.

Some of the people had turned pale with the news they'd received. Others had burst into tears, and one or two had laughed. But the old woman just twitched.

It was as though someone had suddenly stuck her with a pin. She drew a breath, raised her arms, and sent the telephone flying. The string snapped in her fingers, and the beads tumbled all over the floor. Some skittered and bounced under the cabinet, only to roll right back as though thrown by a ghostly hand.

On the floor, the telephone rang. The old woman—now as pale and still as a pile of salt—just stared at it. So her neighbor picked it up, a younger man with hair as red as my mother's. He listened to the voice, then looked up. "It's for Scooter King," he said.

There were many envious looks as the telephone was

passed to me. The lady right at my side, who had still not re-ceived a message, gave me the high hat now, ignoring me completely. The telephone had to be passed *around* her as she sat with her arms crossed, glaring like a wooden Indian.

I put the receiver to my ear. I heard the crackle of elec-tricity, and then a very different voice than I had heard be-fore. "This is your father," it said.

I nearly dropped the receiver. Into my mind sprang a memory that I had forgotten, and I saw the face of my father—in my mind—smiling as he held me, spinning round and round, with everything behind him in a sideways blur.

"Dad!" I said. "Is it really you?"

"Yes, son," he said. "Do you remember me?"

"Sure I do, Dad!"

"Of course. I'm your old Fat Daddy. Remember that, how everyone called me Fat Daddy? Well, I want you to know, son, that you don't have to worry anymore. I'm happy in Summerland. Of course I miss you like crazy, you and your mother, and I always will until we're together again. But lis-ten. I play every night with Ernest Hogan, and . . ."

The voice went on, but I didn't care anymore. It was all fake, just the same stupid story that Mother had spun at the Limelight Club for the loathsome little piano player. I dropped the telephone on the floor and stood up.

Right away, the phone started ringing again.

I kicked it aside. The candlestick part smashed against the leg of a chair. The receiver spun away at the end of its cord, wrapping round and round that leg. The ringing went on and on, and the guy with red hair got down to untangle it all.

I stepped over him. I made my way toward the door, with everyone staring at me. The blue light pulsed in their faces, in their eyes. The Stranger watched me pass.

I hurried for the door. The thought came to me that the old man in the tricycle chair might have locked the door behind him. So I grabbed the handle and threw all my weight against the door.

To my surprise, it opened easily. I went crashing into the hall.

19

Thursday, June 10, 1926

EXTRA! EXTRA!

Boy Finds Hidden Dungeon

I ran down the winding hall toward the front of the house, where I had chased the Stranger only a week ago.

Head down, running, I passed doors on either side, dark alcoves, corridors branching off. I ran straight for the old elevator near the front door. But when I got there, the gate was pulled shut, the elevator gone. Above the empty door, a metal arrow pointed to the left.

There was a big button on the wall. I pushed it hard, and right away I heard the thunk and whine of an electric motor starting up, and the rumble of gears turning. As the arrow

above me swung slowly upright, I saw the roof of the elevator easing up above the floor.

Still gasping breaths, I watched the cage rise in its shaft.

I had never seen an elevator that didn't need a man or
boy to work it. This one seemed to run on magic, because
the cage was empty. Summoned by the push of the button, it
came clanking up from the basement. A boy would have
had to struggle to bring the cage level with the floor, throwing his lever forward and back. But Viktor's elevator lurched
to a stop at the proper place as though a ghost had brought it
there. I opened the gate, went through, and closed it again
behind me.

Inside were more buttons. I pushed one with my thumb,
and the elevator started down.

I descended into a basement that was dark and gloomy.
The elevator lurched on its cables, then settled to a stop below the old castle.

Far away, a blue light glowed in a distant room. It was
the same color as the spirit light that had hovered, pulsing,
over Viktor's cabinet. Everywhere else lay a shadowy darkness filled with the most mysterious things imaginable.
Viktor Valerian couldn't have made his basement more
spooky if he had tried.

I moved toward the light, past a moose head sitting on a
chair. Its antlers cast shadows that looked like enormous
hands, with many fingers reaching out. There was a suit of
armor with only one leg, a skeleton in a glass case. In a

corner stood the coffin of an Egyptian mummy, the lid half open. There was a smell of dirt and the steady drip of water.

I kept looking to either side, turning right around, walking backward now and then. I passed a teetering pile of old books, a stack of steamer trunks.

As I crept closer to the light, I saw that it spilled out through a strange doorway—an oval-shaped hole in a wall of thick cement. The door itself was made of metal and looked very spiffy and expensive. But it was held open by a wooden coat hanger.

To get there, I had to pass through a maze of rickety shelves made of planks and bricks. They stood in row after row, in zigzags and L shapes, towering high above me, all laden with bottles and old glass jars. It seemed that a touch in the wrong place could send the whole works crashing down.

Glints of light caught my eye as I passed along the shelves. I turned anxiously toward each one, but found only reflections on the jars and bottles. The basement was so eerie, so quiet and creepy, that I imagined if I looked inside those jars I would find pickled toes and pickled fingers— horrible blobs of skin with shriveled nails, the white ends of bones still sticking out. I made the image so vivid that, in the end, I *had* to look, just to show myself that I was wrong. So I picked up a jar and turned it to the light.

The jar seemed full of eyeballs! I could see a dozen or more floating in a greenish liquid, turning and rolling, bumping each other. I nearly dropped the jar. I had to fumble to hold on to it, to keep it from smashing on the cement floor. Then I saw the label on the glass, the writing neat and perfect.

Spring Onions
May 17, 1923

My mother's voice came to my mind: *Spooked by a pickle.* I wanted to laugh at myself but couldn't quite manage it.

I went on through the maze of shelves, round the zigzags, until there was only one more that I had to pass. I looked between a pair of bottles, and what I saw made my heart leap to my throat.

On the other side of the shelf, a man was sitting just outside the oval door.

I could see only his legs from the knees down, a pair of black shoes on his feet. Everything else was lost in the darkness.

I pressed against the shelves, forgetting—for a moment—how flimsy they were. The whole stack tilted forward, the jars and bottles tinkling. It trembled to a stop and came rocking back toward me. I tried to steady it all, holding on to the shelves until everything was still.

The man never moved. I could hear the tiny splash of water dripping, and the murmuring voice of Viktor Valerian on the floor above me, asking spirits to appear. I crouched on the floor. On the lowest shelf, cobwebs as thick as curtains encased the bottles in white. I drew them apart, hearing the sticky sizzle of the strands breaking. In the blue glow from the oval door, I saw dead spiders and bugs curled up in the bottles.

Right in front of me was the spoked wheel of the tricycle chair. I thought it was the shriveled old man who sat there waiting, the toes of his shoes nearly touching the bottles.

But when I looked up, I saw that the chair was empty. Above the man's knees was nothing but shadows—as though he had no body, no head or arms or hands. I reached between the bottles and touched the man's legs.

They were made of metal, cold and hard. When I tapped with my knuckles, the sound was like the hollow bong of a child's tin drum. I got up and went round the last set of shelves. I pulled away the man's abandoned blankets and saw that the metal legs were bolted to the front of the tricycle chair.

After years of séances, I believed I had seen every strange thing that could ever be seen. But a shriveled old man who left his legs behind? I wondered if he had oozed away like a snake, or had dragged himself with stubby crocodile arms. My mind made him into a monster, a thing from the dime museum, and I looked around in fear, certain that I would see him creeping—or crawling, or oozing—toward me. I stepped over the sill of that rounded door, into the room where the blue light glowed.

There was nothing mysterious about the light. A single bulb, painted blue, dangled from bare wires on the ceiling.

The paint was beginning to peel away, so the blue was crazed with spidery lines of glaring white.

The room was a dungeon, down below the castle. The walls were made of smooth cement, with not a single window anywhere. Above me was a maze of old water pipes—copper and iron and lead—crossing each other in every direction. One had sprung a leak that someone had tried to patch with a bit of cloth wrapped round and round the pipe. Drops of water oozed through the cloth, bulging on its surface. Each swelled like a tick, then, fattened, let go and fell into a wooden bucket already half full. From end to end, that dungeon was thirty feet long. But other than the oval door, the only opening was a square trap in the ceiling. Its panel was pushed aside; a stepladder stood underneath it.

Beyond the ladder was a row of old wardrobes and cabinets. A wooden table, painted black, was pushed against the wall. It was strewn with mysterious things. But the ladder and the trapdoor were all I needed to put my puzzle together. I understood everything then.

I could hear the Russian right above me now, moaning in his trance. The pulse of his strange light came down through the trap, filling the room every few moments with a watery glow.

I kept close to the walls, circling the stepladder. In the cabinets and wardrobes, I saw exactly what I thought I'd find. Hanging in a row were costumes made of cheesecloth—an Indian chief and a sea captain, Cleopatra and Abraham Lincoln. There were half a dozen reaching rods standing in a bucket, a whole shelf full of tin trumpets, a clutch of balloons wearing paper masks. I saw tambourines and bells, jars of spirit lights, a guitar and a ukulele.

It was almost embarrassing, somehow, to see all at once the secrets of the Bolshevik's spooks. Everything that had flown out of the cabinet—from the telephone to the flowers to the leaves and guitar—had come from this dungeon.

I heard a shuffling sound behind me and the tap of the stepladder rocking on the cement. I looked up in time to see a pair of feet coming down through the trap. Little saddle shoes, white and black, swung in the air, feeling for the top of the ladder.

I knew who would come down through that hole, and I didn't want him to find me in the room. I couldn't get past the ladder to the door, so I scuttled sideways. I hid behind a rack of cheesecloth costumes.

The saddle shoes settled on the ladder and started down the steps. Through the trap, down from Viktor's cabinet, came the piano player from the Limelight Club.

He had to spring down the ladder's steps, dropping from one to the other. Then he crossed the floor in his rolling gait, to the wooden table against the wall. It was covered with electrical switches and dials and gauges, with a speaker and a microphone, all connected by a bundle of wires as thick as my arm. It looked like a snake of colored stripes crawling from a box on the wall. There was an ashtray too, and a cigar box, and a heap of matchbooks.

The dwarf stood up on a wooden box stool. He tapped a

few dials, then flicked a couple of switches. From one, a spark flew out, and his hand jerked back. He looked at his fingertip, where a new little scar must have just appeared. Then he grabbed a cigar and a matchbook, got down from the box, and chose a few things from the rack of cheesecloth costumes. He put them on right away: a smock that he pulled over his head, a pair of thin gloves, and a woman's bonnet with a sort of veil that he pushed aside. He turned himself into the white spirit of a young girl, with the laces of her bonnet dangling. Then he lit his cigar and sat on the bottom step of the ladder. He hiked up his smock, leaned back, and crossed his legs. With his face lifted, he puffed balls of smoke into the blue light.

It was no mystery to me anymore who had killed Herman Day and who had killed Dr. Wiseman. I couldn't prove it yet, but I knew.

The dwarf flicked his ashes onto the floor. Then he bent down, ground out his cigar, and set it carefully on the ladder's step. He arranged the veil so that it covered his face, then straightened his smock and started up the ladder.

He went easily and quickly through the trapdoor. As soon as he vanished, I came out from my hiding place and stood at the foot of the ladder.

20

Thursday, June 10, 1926

EXTRA! EXTRA!

Shifty Dwarf Pulls Fast One

I looked up the steps of the ladder, through the hole in the ceiling, into the cabinet of Viktor Valerian. The hole opened directly under his chair, where the chains and locks had made everything seem so solid. The dwarf was squirming out between the legs of that chair. The blue light cast its dim shadows like tongues of cold fire.

The Russian raised his voice to hide the shuffling sounds of the dwarf. "I feel the presence of a child," he said. "A girl who passed to the other side two years ago tomorrow."

A woman cried out in the séance room. "Emily?" she asked with terrible hopefulness. "Emily, are you there?"

"She is near. Very near," said the Russian.

The dwarf chimed in with a girlish lisp. "Was that my mama?" He sounded frightened and wondering. "Mama, where are you?"

"I'm here, baby," cried the woman.

221

"Mama?"

"Yes. I'm right here. Oh, I've missed you."

I could see the dwarf above me in the cabinet, trying to cover his silly saddle shoes by tugging on his cheesecloth dress. Viktor's hands reached out to adjust the bonnet. Then the dwarf slipped very slowly from the cabinet, gliding out between the curtains. It seemed very black now in the room, and the dwarf shimmered in the weird glow of phosphorescent paint.

I climbed two steps of the ladder, then a third, daring to poke my head through the hole. I was right under the Russian's chair. His heels were just in front of me, his shoes touching together. I could smell his socks.

There was no gap between the cabinet and the floor. What had seemed like empty space from the outside was only an illusion. A solid wall had sent the old woman's beads bouncing back from beneath the cabinet. I knew roughly how it worked; I had seen the same thing in Houdini's vanishing box.

In the room above me, the dwarf was moving around. I could hear the scuffing of his shoes, and then a woman's cry: "My baby, my baby."

I had wanted so badly for Viktor to be real that the truth kind of sickened me now. If Viktor was fake, was *everything* fake? Was there no Summerland, no chance of Mother ever hearing from Pop, no hope in the end for something more than life? I was suddenly angry at the Russian. I felt like climbing through the hole and throwing open the curtains, revealing his sweet little Emily as only a dwarf in a cheese-cloth bonnet.

But I didn't do that. I was afraid of the Russian. I went back down the ladder, feeling sad and angry at the same time, feeling determined as well. I could hardly wait to report back to Houdini.

I looked at the table full of electrical stuff, and it wasn't hard to figure out what everything did. On a wooden box was a row of buttons.

I wondered what the Russian would do if I started pressing the buttons, if his mystical telephone suddenly rang in his séance room. Would he answer? I imagined his whispering voice coming through the speaker, shaking with wonder: *Hello?*

A clattering noise made me turn around. I saw the dwarf's fancy little shoes starting down the ladder again. Suddenly, all I wanted was to be away from there. I had to get out of the room—out of the house—before the dwarf came down and saw me.

But before I could move, someone grabbed me from behind.

It nearly scared the life right out of me. It made me gasp for breath.

A hand reached over my shoulder and clamped on my mouth. I struggled, but whoever held me was strong. He lifted me right off the floor as I kicked and squirmed, and he hauled me across the room, under the crisscrossing pipes, through the oval door. I tried to grab on to something. A stack of shelves tilted, then toppled, shattering jars and bottles.

The dwarf gave a startled cry. It was like the sound of a crow—a caw of surprise. He came rattling down the ladder.

Up in his cabinet, Viktor must have known that something was wrong. His voice came clearly now, through the floor and the trap. "The portal is closing. Everything fades into blackness."

With a rasping of wood and a clank of metal, the trapdoor closed above me.

"That is all. There is no more," said Viktor.

The arm tightened round my neck. I was pulled down into a dark place. A man's voice whispered hoarsely: "Don't make a sound."

I clawed at his hand. I let out gargling cries as I struggled. But the man easily pinned me on the cold floor, as though he was a cowboy and I was a steer to be branded. "Keep still!" he hissed.

I thought I would die if I didn't get his hand away from my mouth, and in my struggles I kicked over a shelf full of bottles. They clinked on the concrete. One of them burst, filling the basement with the smell of vinegar. I saw the dwarf coming toward us.

He swayed and rocked. With his spirit costume glowing, he looked like a demon. He stepped over the broken glass with a crackling from his shoes.

At the same time, at the other end of the basement, Viktor Valerian came tramping down a flight of stairs. He threw a switch on the wall, and a blaze of lights blew away the shadows. In his right hand he held a gun.

The dwarf called out to him, "They're over there. Behind the shelves."

I peered between the baskets and saw Viktor marching toward us, past the moose head and the coffin. He swept aside the baskets, and they tumbled away, rolling and bouncing on the cement floor. He looked down at me.

"So it's you," he said. His Russian accent was suddenly gone. "Come here."

He grabbed my arm and hauled me out. I looked back at the man who had surprised me in the other room. He was standing now, his back against the wall. It was the Stranger.

The dwarf was shouting. "They seen it all. They were right in the room."

Viktor twisted my arm until I winced from the pain. He threw me to the floor and tossed his gun to the dwarf. "Watch him," he said. Then, quick as a cat, he spun round and kicked the Stranger in the stomach. I had never seen anyone strike out so quickly or so hard.

With a groan, the Stranger doubled forward. But Viktor

went at him again, attacking like a boxer. Crouched down, fists blurred, he socked in one blow after another, all rabbit punches to the stomach. The Stranger put up his arms to guard his face, and Viktor kept punching.

I'd thought the Stranger was a strong man; I had feared him. But now he crumpled with hardly a fight. He collapsed to his knees.

Viktor stood over him, breathing heavily. "Ya lousy rat," he said. "Ya lousy, yella rat." His voice was no longer deep and stirring. The Bolshevik—once charming—was just a thug in a good suit. "Why couldn't ya leave me alone? Well, you'll pay for it now, all right."

He grabbed the Stranger by one arm and hauled him through the oval door, into the dungeon. The dwarf, pointing with the gun, herded me after him.

Viktor hurled the Stranger into a corner, into a heap on the floor. "Don't say a word," he said. In his accent, I heard a bootlegger from the Bronx, just as Mother had told me. "Not a *woid*," he said. "Or you'll get more of what I gave ya." Then he glanced at the dwarf. "Get everyone out. Put on the locks, then get the auto ready."

The dwarf gave the gun to Viktor and vanished through the door. Viktor Valerian looked round the room, up at the pipes above him. "Ya know, this is one of the oldest joints in the city," he said. "It was built before the waterwoiks, before the sewers went in. Up here on the hill, folks collected rain from the roofs."

"That's swell," I said. I didn't know why he was giving me the grand tour.

"Of course, we're all on city water now. But this room here, this was the cistern," he said. "A big tank to hold water. That's why there's no windows, see. There wasn't even a door; I put that in myself."

He moved to his left but kept the gun aimed toward me. I heard the wheels of the dwarf's tricycle chair rolling him through the basement. The Stranger, in his corner, didn't move.

"I wonder what the Man in the Moon will say about this," said Viktor. "'Tragedy at medium's house.' Or, 'Curiosity killed the cat burglar.' That's a good one." He laughed, then started rehearsing the story he would tell the police. "'Oh, my, Sergeant Summer, what a terrible tragedy,'" he said, rubbing his hands together. "'I don't understand what that poor boy was after. Nothing in the house could be worth his life.'"

He was standing now under the leaky pipe, beside the bucket that caught the drips. I could see a new drop forming right then, bulging through the cloth patch,

"'How were they to know, Sergeant?' Yes, that's what I'll say," said Viktor, his accent switching back and forth. "'The door only opens from the outside. Oh, I wish I'd thought of putting in an escape mechanism. I never dreamed this would happen.'"

In the corner, the Stranger was watching. He had lost

his glasses, and I could see the weird colors of his eyes, changed again by the darker shadows.

"I'll come back later and 'discover' the bodies," said Viktor. "I'll call the cops right away, of course. I'll be in a terrible fit. 'Oh, dear! Oh, dear!' That's what I'll say. I'll be wringing my hands when the sergeant comes round."

He reached up and took hold of the water pipe. He pulled on it, hard enough that the metal groaned. The leak became bigger, the drops falling more often into the bucket. Another pull, and it broke. Water came out in a roaring rush. It blasted against the wall, knocking aside the Indian costume, twirling the spirit hands on the ends of the reaching rods.

I imagined it filling the room, creeping toward the ceiling. I could picture myself treading water in the darkness, trying to squeeze my mouth into a narrowing space of air.

I was terrified but tried not to show it. "This won't fool the police," I said. "It won't fool anyone. And you'll never get the prize now—not as soon as they see all this stuff."

"Stuff? Oh, you mean my little museum?" The Russian smiled as he gestured round the room. "Sadly, all that Sergeant Summer will see is a lot of flotsam tangled round the bodies, the ruins of a valuable collection."

There was already a pool of water at his feet. A whole river coursed down the wall, and things were beginning to spin and turn in the current. I tried to guess how long it would be until the room was full to the ceiling. I figured on less than an hour.

"Oh, don't look so frightened," said Viktor. "You won't drown. I promise that." He pointed toward the table, with its box of switches and wires. "Electricity, my boy. As I understand it, that box is full of electrical juice, and so are the wires. The moment the water comes over that table . . . *zzzzzt!* That'll be it, boy. Your end will be painless."

I looked at his shoes. The water was lapping over the tops of his toes, rising even more quickly than I'd thought. The Stranger—in his corner—stirred himself from the floor. He got up to his knees, then coughed harshly. He tried to speak through the coughing. "I knew you had an accomplice," he said. "I just didn't expect an evil dwarf."

"Evil?" The Russian laughed heartily. "Oh, no. He's a shifty little fellow, but he isn't evil. Now, I'm sorry, but I must be going."

His feet kicked splashes of water as he headed for the door. I wanted to cry for help, but I knew it would do no good. So I spoke as boldly as I could. "You murdered Herman Day. And Dr. Wiseman, too."

He stopped. "Did I?"

"Yes," I said. "Then you sent your dwarf after me, and *he* killed Mr. Doyle."

"What an imagination you've got," said Viktor. "But even if you're right, it makes no difference."

"You think so?" I asked. "If I could figure it out, so will the police."

"Well, what did you 'figure' exactly?" he asked.

"I know that you went to the Orpheum dressed as an old

man." I started moving sideways, thinking that I could circle past him and reach the door. "You murdered Herman Day, then tipped his body into the Torture Tank."

"Ridiculous!" said Viktor. "I was giving a séance. Three dozen people will swear I never left the cabinet. Besides, I had no reason to kill Herman Day. Why would I want to do that?"

"You didn't *want* to," I said. "You went down there to kill Houdini."

His laugh sounded hollow. "I did?"

"Yes. You had to get Houdini off the prize committee. You had to get him out of the way. You thought you could drown him in his Torture Tank if you jammed one of its locks. So you came down through the trapdoor while everyone thought you were sealed in the cabinet. You picked up a matchbook from the table, a walking stick, a false beard, and white hair. Of course it would be white; all spirit things are. Then you ran down the stairs on the bluff, and at the bottom you put on your disguise."

He looked at me but didn't say anything. I moved a bit closer to the door.

"Your plan almost worked," I said. "But Herman Day came into the room while you were jamming the lock. You panicked."

"I never panic," said the Russian. But he did look worried.

The water surged through the pipe, spraying from the

wall. A set of spirit hands floated past the Russian's feet and seemed to grab on to his ankle. He kicked them away.

"You probably told Herman to climb up and look in the tank," I said. "And when he did, you bashed him from behind."

That was only a guess, but from the expression on Viktor's mug, I knew it was right on the money.

"There's no evidence," he said.

"I found the beard."

"Where?"

"In the gutter behind the Orpheum." I didn't tell him the rest of the story—that I'd mistaken the scraggly bit of white hair for a cat's tail and left it where it was.

Viktor licked his lips "Well, maybe I did go to the Orpheum. But so what?" he said. "Maybe I wanted to see the great Houdini and his Burmese Torture Tank. Maybe I found Herman Day jamming the lock. How about *that*? I surprised him as he was trying to jam the lock. So of course I tried to stop him. I couldn't help myself; I just hit him, and—well, if you think about it, I'm a hero."

"No, you're a liar," I said. "And they'll know it, because there's one thing you *didn't* see."

"What's that?"

"Herman Day needed glasses."

The Russian frowned.

"He wore cheaters," I said. "I saw them in his dressing room, on the counter. They were thick as bottles, so he must have been half blind without them. He couldn't possibly have seen how to jam that lock. He could hardly have seen the *lock*. So there was no chance he would have recognized you in your fake beard. You killed him for nothing."

"Oh, what a shame." The water was now above Viktor's ankles. He shifted from one foot to the other, like a heron in a pond. "You're clever, kid. But too bad you won't be around to explain it all to the cops. Somehow I don't think that Sergeant Summer has the same imagination."

From above us, through the trapdoor, came a rattle of chains and locks. It was a mysterious sound that made me remember something that Mother had told me. She'd heard the same thing—"this clanking, like ghostly chains"—at the end of Viktor's séance. It must have been the sound of the medium coming up into his cabinet after killing Herman Day. Now I knew it was the sound of the dwarf closing that same trapdoor. I heard his hurried footsteps as he dashed out of the cabinet.

To my left, a tambourine floated out of the shadows, rocking in the surge of water. It bumped against the ladder, its little cymbals jingling, and spun away on the current. Viktor kicked it aside as he waded toward the door.

"You came to the séance at the Orpheum planning to kill me," I said. "You freed yourself from the circle, and you did a little tap dance so that everyone would think my mother had raised the spirit of Herman Day. Your dwarf had met Herman at the Limelight Club, so you knew his expressions. '*Hello, Central . . .*' You're good at imitations, at

accents. But you didn't figure that I would change places with Dr. Wiseman or that Houdini would bring a camera. When he caught you with his flash, you knew you had to destroy the picture."

"All right," said Viktor Valerian. "You figured it out. You cracked the case." He bowed in his courtly way. "But what good does it do you? Think of your poor mother. Why, she'll be devastated when she gets the news of your death. I may have to go and comfort her myself."

His accent changed again, to an Englishman's now. "Well, cheerio," he said, waggling his fingers in a saucy wave. "Chin up, old boy." He stepped back through the door. He slammed it shut.

I heard the handle spin, the lock engage. I hurled myself against the door, but of course it didn't budge. I could only stand there, in the blue light of that dungeon, and watch the water rising.

21

EXTRA! EXTRA!

MYSTERY MAN REVEALED

I knocked over the racks, spilling gauzy clothes and speaking trumpets. I tore at wood and metal until I had a bar to pry with. Then I attacked the door.

From either side, from up and down, I pulled and hammered at the metal. But nothing budged. So I went up the ladder instead and tried to push my way through the trap.

It was made of two parts that were joined in the middle. I jiggled both sides and forced a small gap between them. But they wouldn't budge beyond that; they were locked firmly in place.

From his corner of the room, the Stranger finally spoke. "Do you know what we need?"

"What?" I asked, looking down from the ladder.

"I'll tell you," he said. "What we need just now is Harry Houdini."

"Yeah, that's swell," I said. "Thanks a lot."

I thought it was a terrible time for the Stranger to go on a laughing jag. But off he went, chuckling away to himself. He put his hands to his face, as though to smother his laughter. His fingers poked at his eyes. Suddenly, he tipped his head forward.

I wondered if he was going to collapse. The beating he had taken would have left most men curled on the floor, groaning in pain.

But not the Stranger.

He prodded and pulled at his eyes. Then he raised his head again—and he was a different person. In his hands were tiny saucers of tinted glass. Without those lenses, his eyes were as blue as oceans.

He shoved the saucers in his pocket, then reached up and pulled off his silvery hair. He dropped the wig in the water, ripped away his eyebrows and gray mustache.

"Mr. Houdini!" I said.

Underneath the Stranger's wig, behind those glasses and the mumbling voice, was the magician himself. He smiled at me now. "Let me up on the ladder, Scooter. We haven't a minute to lose."

I leapt down and gave him my place. He braced his huge arms on the side of the hole and pushed at the panels with all his strength. But no matter how he struggled, he could widen the gap by only an inch.

"He's got it locked from above," said Houdini. He worked his fingers through the open end and felt along its

edge. I heard a rattle of metal. "Yes; it's almost hopeless. Well, never mind."

He came down, then surged past me in the rising water, through the rafts of floating debris. With all the spirit clothes and ghostly faces drifting in the blue light, it looked as though the *Titanic* had gone down in the room.

Houdini leaned against the wall. He put his hands to the door—like a doctor to a patient—and began to tap and poke.

The water kept bubbling and boiling up the wall. It rose over Houdini's trouser cuffs, up along his calves. But it seemed that he wasn't even aware of it. Patiently, quietly, he examined the door. The water was nearly at his knees when he finally spoke.

"This is a Schliebermachen," he said. "Type three, if I'm not mistaken. Do you know they were only made in a seven-month period in 1917? They're so rare that this is actually the first one I have ever seen. The German navy used them as escape hatches in its submarines, so of course they were never meant to be opened from this side."

"Then how do you open it?" I asked.

"From the other side." He gave me a wonderful smile, full of his old charm. "No, it's quite impossible to open a Schliebermachen. We can't get out this way."

Well, there was only one *other* way. It was the locked panel at the top of the ladder.

"Back we go," said Houdini.

The water was deep enough now that the ladder was trying to float. In the swirling current it lifted one leg at a time and lurched across the floor like some sort of crazy wading machine. Houdini wrestled it back into place. In a flash, he was halfway to the top. He got his fingers through the gap again and started groping like a blind man. His head was turned aside, jammed against the ceiling, and the tip of his tongue was sticking out.

I looked at the table with its wires and electrical box. The water was now a foot and a half from the top. Just eighteen inches, and then . . . *zzzzzt!* That would be it.

"Well, I can feel the lock," said Houdini, on the ladder. "It's hard to reach, but I can do it. We could try to pry the panels apart, but I bet we'd be at it all day. Better to pick the lock, I think."

"Okay. Sure," I said. I leaned forward on the ladder, resting while Houdini did the work. I figured picking a lock was as easy as pie for Harry Houdini.

The water was inching up the legs of the table, but I wasn't worried. What luck to be locked in a room with the one man in the whole world who could escape from anything. Houdini had freed himself from jail cells and straitjackets, from coffins in the earth, and from caskets in the water. What was a concrete cistern compared to any of that? I figured we'd be out in a sec.

"Mr. Houdini?" I said. "When Viktor was giving you the business, why didn't you fight back? You could have knocked his lights out if you wanted to, couldn't you?"

"Easily. I could have managed that with one hand. Blindfolded," he said, still fiddling with the lock. "But do you think it would have been wise?"

"Sure," I said. "You beat the automaton, didn't you? And Dr. Yu, and Dr. Strange, and—"

"Those were the moving pictures," said Houdini. "If there's one thing I've learned through trial and error, it's this: when a crazy man comes at you with a gun, it's best to do as he says."

"But gee, Mr. Houdini . . ." I could hear my voice squeaking again. "I saw you catch a bullet in your teeth."

"You thought you did." Houdini smiled down from the ladder. "Believe me, I have the upper hand on that Bolshevik."

"But you let him park you on your tail," I said. "You let him beat Houdini."

"Not at all." He paused in his work, bringing down his hands to flex his fingers. The skin was turning purple. "Viktor thought he was giving a beating to Mr. Brown, an old socks with silver hair and spectacles. He has no idea that Harry Houdini is on to him now, and I didn't want him to find out in a dingy basement. When I expose that scoundrel, I want the world to be there, Scooter. I think I might do it on the courthouse steps, with all the newshounds and the cameras and the Man in the Moon looking up at me. Yes, that would be good."

He nodded to himself, then again shoved his hands into the gap. I heard the rattle of the lock as he twisted it around.

My seconds had turned to minutes. The water had risen another step on the ladder, and it was still blasting from the pipe. Bouquets of celluloid flowers started floating round my legs. The water was eight inches from the tabletop when Houdini called down, "Scooter, can you do me a favor?"

"What?" I said. We had to raise our voices over the roar of water.

"Find something long and skinny. Like a bit of wire."

"Okay," I said.

"But not too soft. Nothing bendy."

Well, that was easy. I imagined it was Houdini's turn now to feel lucky. He had found himself in a locked room with someone who knew an awful lot about wire. I had rigged so many spirit hands, so many tilting tables, and rappers and tappers, that I was an expert on the stuff.

I sorted through all the junk that floated in the room. I found the Indian headdress and plucked its artificial feathers. From each I pulled a length of stiff wire, and in a moment I was passing them up to Houdini.

He took them without looking, rolling them in his fingers. "Hmmm," he said. "We'll need another piece as well. Something flat-sided."

I saw the water rising up the table and wished Houdini wasn't quite so fussy. For the first time, I thought we might not make it out.

It was now hard to walk—the water was so deep. I had to lean forward and push myself with my feet. Everything I bumped against, I tore apart. There were reaching rods and rubber hands, a pair of shoes with hollow heels. I ripped through yards of gauze, through masks and hats and crinolines. Then I stood on something that rolled underneath my foot and sent me falling backward. I sank into the water over my head, got up, and surged forward again. I felt with my feet now, sensing the crunch of broken glass, until I found what had tripped me. Then I ducked down to pick it up, the roar of water from the pipe turning to a different sort of rumble in my ears. I came up, shook the water from my hair, and looked at the speaking trumpet in my hands.

Its metal was soft and pliable, its round end stiffened by a circle of wire. I bashed the trumpet against the ladder; I crushed it in my hands. Then Houdini snatched it up, and tore out the wire with his fingers and teeth.

"Perfect," he said when he saw it.

He went to work on the lock, trying to squeeze his hands through the gap. Already he had torn the skin from his knuckles and a nail from a finger, but he tried again. He fumbled with the wire, and it fell from his hand.

I saw the splash. I caught the wire as it sank. When I passed it up again, I had to put it in his hand. It was as though he had no feeling anymore.

"This damned lock's a Monte Cristo," he said. I could hear the frustration in his voice. "Anything else I'd have open by now. But a Monte's tricky."

Again he dropped the wire. It pinged off the ladder and vanished underwater.

"Damn!" said Houdini. "That was the round one. Scooter, I need another feather."

There were a lot of things floating now. The whole surface of the water—the whole room—was a mass of bubbling gauze and bits of junk. I wasted another minute or two searching through it, and by the time Houdini had the wire, the water was less than six inches from the electrical juice. The end wasn't far off.

Houdini too looked at the electrical wires, at the box fixed to the table. He brought down his hands, and I saw that big patches of skin were scraped away. When he went back to work, his hands were shaking, and he was wincing with pain. I couldn't tell if the drips that fell from his forehead were water or sweat.

"I can't do it!" he shouted suddenly. In his anger, he nearly threw away the wire. "It's no damned good. There's no room for my hands."

"What about mine?" I asked. They were smaller. "If you tell me how, I'll pick the lock."

"A Monte? You haven't a chance," said Houdini.

"There's no *other* chance," I said.

There wasn't room for both of us on one step of the ladder. Houdini came down, red and cursing, and I went up in his place. I held out my hand for the wire, but he wouldn't give it to me.

"Find the lock first," he said. "Touch it. Feel it."

Even I had to squeeze my hands through that gap. There was room for my wrists, but no more. The wood pinched my arm like a vise. I felt along the space, back and forth, until I found the lock.

It was much bigger than any lock I'd seen, a square chunk of metal that seemed to weigh three pounds. I could feel the keyhole easily.

"What do you know about locks?" asked Houdini.

"Not much," I said.

"Well, there's a tumbler inside. It's called a plug, and it's the part that revolves when you turn the key," he said. "There are two rows of metal pins, one in the body and one in the plug. When the lock's engaged, the pins line up, and a set of springs pushes the pins in the body down on the ones in the plug. When you insert the key, you push up the pins and free the plug. Understand?"

"No," I said. "Could you tell me again? In English?"

I didn't mean to, but I made him angry. Maybe he thought I was bugging him because he was born in Hungary, because he wasn't really American. All I knew was that he suddenly looked furious.

"Like this!" he shouted. With the wire, he scraped a little picture into the wooden step of the ladder.

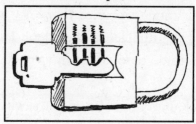

"You have to push up the pins," he said. "These pins here!" He stabbed at his picture. "Use the square wire to turn the lock. Use the round one to rake it."

"What do you mean?" I asked.

"Here!" He slapped the wires into my hand. "Shove the round one into the keyhole, right to the back of the plug. Get it in line with the pins, or you won't do any good. Use the square one to turn the lock. Firmly, but not too hard! Then drag the round wire over the pins. Do it fast. You want to push the pins out of the plug."

I thought I understood. It sounded easy, but doing it was hard.

"Don't rush yourself," said Houdini. "Use the round wire first and find the pins. They won't stick out very far, but you can feel them move up and down when you touch them."

Reaching over my head, working blindly, I had enough trouble just getting the wire into the hole. And then to feel the pins? It seemed impossible. The wire shook in my hand.

"Feel it. Feel it!" said Houdini.

I stood just as he had stood, with my head pressed against the ceiling. I could see the water swirling round the ladder, nearly touching the bottom of the tabletop.

"Concentrate," said Houdini. "There's seven pins in that lock. You want to bounce them up, and trap them on the edge of the tumbler so they don't fall down again. And you have to do it to all seven at once. Can you feel the pins?"

"Yes, I think so," I said. The tip of the wire jarred against them. I could drag it down the row, and feel the tiny *tick-tick-tick* as the wire leapt from pin to pin.

"Try pushing them up," said Houdini. "Get the feel of it."

The wire just bounced off the pins, ricocheting all through the lock. But I kept working at it, and I was used to doing things in darkness, by feel alone, so I got better at it as I went along.

"Now the square wire," said Houdini. "Work it into the hole, underneath the round wire."

That was the easiest step. "Okay," I said.

"Now turn the tumbler. But be careful!" said Houdini. "If you turn too hard, you can't push up the pins. But if you don't turn hard enough, you won't catch them."

"Okay."

"And don't ease off!" he cried. "As soon as you've done it, feel for the pins again. See if you've caught them."

I did as he said, jamming the square wire into the key hole, raking the other one down the row of pins. I felt the tumbler turn ever so slightly. All but two of the pins were firmly lodged at the top of the tumbler.

"I got five!" I shouted.

"Good for you," said Houdini. He squeezed my leg with his hand, such a friendly gesture that I suddenly found a second memory of my father. It came in a flash—a whole picture with sound and light and smell and movement. I was climbing a tree, and my father was below me. He was helping me up, but ready to catch me if I fell. I felt the warm wind and the sway of the tree. I saw the clouds scud by; smelled the apples in the tree.

But Houdini shattered the picture. "Move it!" he shouted. "Don't give up now."

The sixth pin went up quite easily. I caught it on the edge of the plug and started on the last pin. But the wire kept slipping off.

"You've got to hurry," said Houdini.

The sound of the water had changed. *All* the sounds had changed. With the room so full, and filling fast, there was a steady wind whistling up through the cracked-open panel.

"Don't force it," said Houdini. "But don't ease off either, or you're back where you started."

I took a long breath to steady myself. My arms were aching, my hands nearly numb. There was a tingling in my wrists where they rested on the edge of the panel.

I tried once more. I put the tip of the wire against the pin. I levered up as I turned the plug. I couldn't hear any sounds from the lock, but I sort of felt a click inside it. The flat wire turned in my hand, and the lock fell open.

"I did it!" I said

"Work it free from the hasp," said Houdini.

The ladder shook as he came up beside me. He nearly knocked us both into the water as he heaved and rattled at the panel. I turned the lock; I pushed and pulled, and somehow it came free. The panel slid aside, opening one half of the trap door. When I put my head through the hole, I saw that the other panel was locked as securely as the first one. Our hole was maybe big enough for a boy to get through, but Houdini wouldn't have a chance.

"Go!" he shouted, pushing at my leg.

I had to squirm under the chair, through the web of Viktor's chains. Houdini tried to help by pushing harder and harder. "The water's rising," he said, not quite as calm anymore. "Go out arms first. Keep your head down and make like a corkscrew."

That was exactly how I did it—twisting from my stomach to my back, bending between the wooden legs of the chair. I scraped the skin from my arms and put ugly bruises on my legs. But I got out. I stood in the cabinet and looked down at Houdini.

"I can't fit," he said. "It's impossible."

His feet were under water. Mats of gauze were floating below him, and the first fingers of water were reaching over the top of the table, feeling across its surface. The thought struck me that I could leave Houdini there if I wanted, or make him bargain for his life. I could have him swear that my mother was a genuine medium, deserving of the *Scientific American* prize. Then I saw him looking up at me, and I was ashamed of the thought. Without a word, I turned around and ran for the basement.

The elevator was waiting. It seemed to take forever to lower me down. I threw the gate aside, then sprinted through the maze of weird and baffling things. I toppled cabinets and caskets and shelves. I knocked over the moose head and sent the skeleton scattering. When I came to the Schliebermachen door, I didn't think twice. I turned the handle.

Water spurted out, and the door flew open, slamming against me. The blast of water hurled me right around as I clung to the handle, so my back smashed against the wall.

A torrent came roaring from the room. It shattered all the shelves and all the bottles, while the spirit hands and gauzy clothes and all the things in the room tumbled and spun.

Then out came Houdini. He was soaking wet, of course, dripping all over, like a dog wading out of a river. He shook himself.

Then he shook my hand.

22

FRIDAY, JUNE 11, 1926

No End in Sight for Rising Stocks
Gasoline Steady at 35 Cents a Gallon
Local Boy Makes Good

Harry Houdini told me not to go blabbing about the things that had happened in Viktor's basement. That was the first thing he mentioned, before we summoned the police, before we got the manhunt started.

"What happened here, it's going to be a matter for the courts," he said. "We shouldn't even discuss it between ourselves."

I promised to keep it secret. But I knew that Houdini wasn't thinking of courts and lawyers. He just didn't want to be embarrassed. He didn't want people to know that the world's greatest escape artist had been saved by a boy. Who could blame him for that?

I kept my promise, but somehow—I could guess how— the Man in the Moon got wind of the story. He wrote about me and Houdini unmasking the Russian. But for once his facts weren't right. The headline on his column said:

He made it out that Houdini was a big hero who had freed us both from a locked room. The way he told it, Houdini had held his breath for seven minutes as he swam around under water, looking for the tools that he needed to pick the locks. He made me look like a real palooka: *Boy clings to ladder with death grip, cries out, "Save me, Houdini!"* I might almost have found it funny, except that everyone believed the story—all except for my mother.

Seven days later, I went down to the Orpheum for Houdini's last performance. Mother wouldn't go with me. She said she couldn't bear to watch him in the Torture Tank. "I don't want to see anybody trapped under water ever again," she said.

After the show was over, after Houdini took his bazillion encores, I went down to the Limelight Club with tiny Bess. Walking beside her, even I looked tall, so the coin-flipping guy didn't say a word. Bess went straight to a table full of people, while I sat by myself in the darkest corner.

There was a three-piece band playing ragtime tunes. I watched the dancers hop and bop around the floor, the girls kicking high, their fringed skirts flapping.

Houdini arrived a bit later, while the band was resting. The joint seemed quiet, though—really—it roared with voices and laughter.

Houdini stood for a moment in the doorway. His face was still white with makeup, so he looked like a vampire coming into the room. He strutted between the tables, striking poses at every one. When he saw me in the corner, he got all loud and happy. "Ah, Scooter King!" he said, so loudly that everyone turned to look. He roared away as he came toward me. "My biggest fan, according to the papers. Me, a hero? What nonsense!" He laughed. "It was nothing, really." Then he put his hand on my shoulder, leaned down, and whispered in my ear.

"I'm surprised to see you," he said. "What's on your mind?"

"Paul Revere," I said.

"Pardon me?"

"You came to our séance. The one with Paul Revere."

"Oh, that!" He laughed very softly, as though suddenly remembering an old joke. "Yes, that was one of the most entertaining nights of my life. I heard you dashing in and out of the wardrobe, and I thought, 'Now there's a boy with gumption.'"

"You sent me a card the next day."

"I did indeed," said Houdini.

"So why didn't you let on that you'd been there?" I said. "When you met me later, why didn't you say something?"

"Oh, I don't know." Houdini slipped into a chair beside me. He took out his handkerchief and started wiping off his makeup. "I never met a medium quite like your mother. She struck me as utterly charming, fresh as a daisy. I got the impression that she believed in herself, that she thought she had real powers."

"That's true," I said.

"I didn't doubt she was in it for the money. She didn't exactly give away her 'talents.' But I could see that she had morals. And that's unusual." Houdini folded the handkerchief and dabbed at his forehead. "Then, of course, there was you. It impressed me how quickly you found the things in my overcoat pockets, how well you pieced them together. Every other medium in the city concluded that Annie was a woman, but you had doubts, didn't you? You were more careful. I saw that, and said to myself, 'Now, there's a boy I can use.' You do still want to be in my secret service, don't you?"

"Oh, yes, sir," I said.

"Good. You'll be my detective. My spirit detective."

The three men in the band were going back to their places. Around the tables, women were looking up eagerly, already rising from their places. They were like cats stirring at the sound of an icebox.

"Mr. Houdini, can I ask you a question?" I said.

He nodded. "Shoot."

"The first time I saw you at Viktor's, I followed you out of the séance room. Where did you go?"

"Upstairs," said Houdini. "I suspected the Bolshevik had a confederate, and I went looking for him on the floor above. Oh, I know the elevator indicated that the cage was in the basement, but I thought it was a ruse. You might say that I outsmarted myself."

Houdini stood up. He had never really thanked me for what I'd done—and he still didn't thank me now—

but he put his hand on my shoulder again, and made me a promise.

"I won't expose your mother," he said. "You have my word."

With that he turned things around, so that *I* should do the thanking. And he acted very humble when I did, waving me off with a little shake of his hand. "Your mother's in the minor leagues," he said. "I can let it go."

I left the Limelight Club and started home. At the end of the block, a newsie was shouting headlines about Viktor Valerian. The medium had been captured, along with the dwarf, at a Shell station in Arkansas. The papers said they would hang for sure, on account of them killing three people.

But it didn't happen.

The next day, somewhere north of Tennessee, the pair escaped from the paddy wagon. The guard who was with them said he couldn't explain how it happened. "It was impossible," he said. "The door was locked. The key was in my pocket."

People hinted that the guard had helped them, but nobody ever proved it. Over the next few months, reports came in that Viktor had been sighted in Florida, or out in California, or just about anywhere in between. A priest in New York said he'd seen the Russian lugging a big box up the gangway of a ship that was casting off for Europe. Wherever he was seen, it was without his beard. My mother said he must have shaved it off, but I figured it was fake—just like everything else about him. He hadn't covered his black beard with a white one on the day of the murder; he had never had a beard at all.

The flurry of sightings lasted ten months. Then people stopped caring. Then people stopped seeing him, except for once a year, when the Man in the Moon did a story about "the vanishing Bolshevik" or "the missing medium" and put in a picture of Viktor, looking like the devil with that black, pointed beard.

Other than that, everything worked out pretty well for my mother and me. She was famous, in a way. Oh, not like John Scopes was famous, or like Captain Amundsen or Josephine Baker. But round the city, everyone knew of Madam King. A lot of people came to see her, and a whole lot more made out that they knew her, like it was a big deal to be a friend of my mother. I was proud of myself for the way it worked out. When it came to solving puzzles, I figured that I was a lot better than Sergeant Summer.

So our séances got pretty crowded sometimes. There were the usual kooks and crackpots, the old birds, and a few spiffy cats. Now and then a new puzzle appeared, in the form of a man with a metal face or a lady who burst into tears of blood. Best of all was the Hangman—who came seven weeks in a row and never spoke a word, always wearing the same black hood.

In the months that followed, I did a bit of spirit detecting for Harry Houdini, following strange instructions that arrived by mail. But it didn't last very long. On Halloween night I was working on one of his cases when I heard on the radio that Houdini had died in Detroit. The horrible dwarf and Dr. Wiseman had been proven right.

Every newspaper had a story; it was even in "The Man in the Moon." They all said the same thing: up in Montreal, a college kid had socked Houdini too hard in the stomach, bursting his appendix.

"Don't you believe it," said Mother. "I think the spirits killed him. That's what I think."

I believe this story was started by fairies. More correctly, it began with *pictures* of fairies, the famous photographs taken by two young girls near the English village of Cottingley.

Frances Griffiths, nine years old, and her cousin Elsie Wright, sixteen, took their first photo in 1917, beside a stream near Elsie's house. Over time, they took four more: three of fairies, and one of a funny little goblin with skinny legs and a pointed hat.

The pictures were beautiful, though the fairies looked silly. It seemed obvious that Frances and Elsie had hung cutout drawings in the bushes by the stream. But in 1920, a lot of people thought the pictures were real, including Sir Arthur Conan Doyle, creator of the fabulously logical Sherlock Holmes.

I became curious how an intelligent man could be swayed by paper cutouts. So I started reading about the photographs, and then about Sir Arthur. He was a spiritualist, his wife a medium who took dictation from the dead, producing pages of automatic writing while sitting in a trance. Inspired by Frances and Elsie, he wrote a book, *The Coming of the Fairies*, claiming that fairies were real. His beliefs brought him ridicule, but Sir Arthur never wavered. In the end I felt very sorry for a kindly old writer who could believe in a lot of things, but not that girls would tell a lie.

Sir Arthur was so entranced by the pictures of the Cottingley fairies that he offered them to Harry Houdini, who had gone to Europe in search of a genuine medium, or at least of a genuine photograph of spirits. Houdini wasn't interested in pictures of fairies, but he became a close friend of Sir Arthur.

How Sir Arthur could be friends with Harry Houdini was almost as baffling as how he could believe in the Cottingley fairies. While Houdini was skeptical of all things spiritual, Sir Arthur could convince *himself* of almost anything. He even came to the startling conclusion that Houdini himself was a medium, performing his famous escapes from locked rooms and underwater boxes by dissolving his body into atoms.

Sir Arthur arranged a séance with his wife and Houdini. Mrs. Conan Doyle went into her trance and channeled pages of automatic writing from the spirit of Houdini's mother. Sir Arthur thought Houdini was impressed. But he was wrong. When Houdini denied that he had found a genuine medium in Mrs. Conan Doyle, it brought an end to the friendship. The men who had been so close became most bitter enemies.

Houdini went off on a crusade against fraudulent mediums. He joined the committee set up by *Scientific American* magazine to seek out mediums with supernatural powers and reward them with prizes. He set up his own "secret service," sending agents to séances, dragging frauds into court. He added a segment to his stage show in which he performed— in bright light—the same tricks that the mediums pulled in the darkness. He wrote a book describing them: *Miracle Mongers and Their Methods*. And wherever he went, he put out a challenge to mediums and exposed them from the stage.

Houdini's book introduced me to the world of spiritual fakery. I loved reading the old accounts of séances and learning the tricks of the mediums. Some were as simple as sliding a finger across a tabletop to make the sound of spirit raps. The most sophisticated tricks involved secret panels in walls and confederates in adjoining rooms. The mediums used false shoes and false hands, balloons and cheesecloth and telescoping rods. Companies were formed to supply luminous paint and spirit-writing slates. A sort of psychic convention was held every year, where mediums gathered to trade information.

The Séance is based on these things I learned. While the story is fiction, its parts are factual. The background behind Scooter and Madam King is a mosaic made of shards of truth. There really was a *Scientific American* committee that included Houdini, and it almost awarded a prize to a medium from Boston. Mina Crandon, known as Margery, convinced most of the committee that she had supernatural powers. She didn't convince Houdini, though, and in the end he exposed her as a fraud.

But even today, there are people who suggest that Houdini cheated. He built a wooden cabinet to contain the medium and challenged her to ring a bell that she couldn't possibly reach. In a trance, in the voice of her spirit control, Margery began to rage against Houdini. She accused him of planting something in the cabinet, so that no matter what happened, she would be accused of trickery. When Margery was released, a folding ruler was found on the cabinet's floor. She and Houdini each swore that the other must have put it there.

Margery wasn't the only medium to cause problems for an investigator. Some were never shown to be frauds at all, like the famous Leonora Piper.

In Houdini's early days, while he was passing himself off as a mystic in small-town opera houses, Mrs. Piper was astounding scientific investigators in England and America. Houdini used cheap tricks to make it seem that he could read people's minds. Mrs. Piper just sat in her living room and told visitors things that were known by no one alive except the visitors themselves. She turned skeptics into believers.

Among her converts was the brilliant William James, a psychologist and founder of the American Society for Psychical Research. James compared his search for a true medium to the challenge of proving that not all crows were black. It was not necessary to show that all mediums were frauds, just as there was no need to demonstrate that all crows were white. Just one genuine medium—or one white crow—would do the job. Over time, as she faced test after test, Mrs. Leonora Piper became known as the white crow.

The story of Mrs. Piper, William James, and the Society for Psychical Research was told best in a book by Deborah Blum: *The Ghost Hunters: William James and the Scientific Search for Proof of Life After Death*. I was surprised how many eerie stories there were of unexplained things, such as curtains that billowed in a room with no wind, or mediums who seemed to be truly in touch with the dead. It changed the way I thought about mediums and séances; it made me think again about everything I'd learned.

Even the Cottingley fairies turned out to be not as simple as they'd seemed at first. In the 1980s, Frances and Elsie gave their last interview about the photographs that had become so famous. Elsie said the pictures were fakes, the fairies only paper cutouts, just as they seemed. But Frances said that only four of the five photographs were faked, and that one was real. She insisted until the end that she had really seen fairies at Cottingley.

acknowledgments

A lot of people helped with the writing of this book. I would like to thank them all, but especially Kathleen Larkin of the Prince Rupert Library; Françoise Bui of Delacorte Press; Bruce Wishant of Prince Rupert, B.C.; Darlene Mace and Mo Olsen of Gabriola Island; the staff of the Gabriola Island branch of the Vancouver Island Regional Library; my partner, Kristin Miller; my parents, Raymond and Margaret Lawrence; and everyone who told me about their supernatural experiences.

about the author

Iain Lawrence studied journalism in Vancouver, British Columbia, and worked for small newspapers in the northern part of the province. He settled on the coast, living first in the port city of Prince Rupert and now on the Gulf Islands. His previous novels include the High Seas Trilogy: *The Wreckers*, *The Smugglers*, and *The Buccaneers*; and the Curse of the Jolly Stone Trilogy: *The Convicts*, *The Cannibals*, *and The Castaways*; as well as *Gemini Summer*, *B for Buster*, *Lord of the Nutcracker Men*, *Ghost Boy*, and *The Lightkeeper's Daughter*.

You can find out more about Iain Lawrence at www.iainlawrence.com.